"Is it mine?" Adam asked.

"No." The denial shot like a bullet through the air.

He knew Eve well enough to feel confident that the child was his no matter what she said to the contrary. The time to back away, to pretend she'd never been part of his life, was over. Eve and their unborn child were at risk. They needed his protection.

"Is this why you left?" he asked, his eyes indicating her swollen abdomen. "Because you found out you were pregnant?"

"No," she retorted hotly. "I left because I found out that you were a drug dealer."

Dear Reader,

I've always felt that Thanksgiving gets lost in the shuffle between Halloween and Christmas. When I was a kid, Thanksgiving was a big deal. There were TV specials, greeting card commercials, even a cartoon special featuring the voice of Tennessee Ernie Ford. Now, as soon as the ghosts and goblins get put away, Santa takes over. While I adore Christmas probably more than the average person, I do think that Thanksgiving needs to be given its due, which is why I've included it in this book. It's not the main focus, but it's in the background, waiting until you have a free moment to spare, like a warm, understanding friend who takes no offense at being ignored because that's how life has arranged itself.

This book is also about secret agents and spies because, let's face it, wouldn't we all love to have them in our lives as long as they were sexy and did no harm to anything but the sheets? I hope you enjoy the journey I take you on and, as ever, I thank you for reading and more than anything, I wish you someone to love who loves you back.

Marie Ferrarella

MARIE FERRARELLA

The Agent's Secret Baby

Silhouette®

Romantic

SUSPENSE

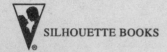

SILHOUETTE BOOKS

Recycling programs for this product may not exist in your area.

ISBN-13: 978-0-373-27650-9

THE AGENT'S SECRET BABY

Copyright © 2009 by Marie Rydzynski-Ferrarella

Visit Silhouette Books at www.eHarlequin.com

Printed in U.S.A.

Books by Marie Ferrarella

MARIE FERRARELLA

This *USA TODAY* bestselling and RITA® Award-winning author has written more than two hundred books for Silhouette Books, some under the name Marie Nicole. Her romances are beloved by fans worldwide. Visit her Web site at www.marieferrarella.com.

To
David McCallum
who, as Illya Kuryakin
in *The Man from U.N.C.L.E.*,
is responsible
for my falling in love with
secret agents and black turtleneck sweaters

Chapter 1

It took her a second to realize that the sigh she heard echoing in the small, converted bedroom that served as her office was her own.

Lost in thoughts of the past and preoccupied, Dr. Eve Walters had thought that the deep sigh had come from Tessa, the German shepherd she'd rescued from a sadistic owner a little more than two years ago. On occasion Tessa, currently curled up under her desk, was given to sighing just like a human being. Considering the life she'd led both B.R.—before rescue—and A.R.—after rescue—the sighs were more than merited. Before, Eve was certain, the dog's sighs had been of the fearful, hopeless variety while now, with Tessa's weight a third more than what it had been when she'd first been rescued, the German shepherd's sighs sounded as if she was exceedingly content with her new life and just couldn't believe her good fortune.

Lately, Eve had become aware of sighing a great deal herself, as if she couldn't catch her breath. And couldn't believe the twists and turns that had brought her to this point.

She supposed she could just shrug her shoulders and attribute her deeps sighs to the fact that she wasn't accustomed to carrying around this much weight, but if she were being honest, the cause for her sighs went a great deal deeper. Never in her wildest dreams did Eve think she would find herself in this position: approaching thirty in a few months, single, alone and very, very pregnant.

Tears suddenly gathered in her eyes and she held them back by sheer will. God, but she was emotional lately. Well, she *was not* going to cry. She wasn't.

Another sigh escaped.

How in heaven's name had she come to this state?

Okay, she was gregarious and fun-loving, but never, ever would anyone have called her reckless. She was always known as the stable one, the one everyone else turned to in times of crisis.

When her mother, Evelyn, had died suddenly on Eve's second day of middle school, Eve was the one who was there for her veterinarian father, Warren, and her older sister, Angela—not the other way around. This while she secretly yearned for someone to comfort *her.* But she couldn't indulge herself, couldn't sink into self-pity no matter how much she wanted to. Others depended on her. And she always came through.

Beneath her genial, warm smile she was the living

embodiment of the old adage, "Look before you leap." Not only did she look, she would take out a surveyor's level and plot every single step from there to here each and every time. It wasn't that she didn't like surprises; she just didn't like being caught unaware. And it certainly wasn't like her to give in to impulse and allow herself to be so completely swept away, especially by a man she'd hardly known.

A man she didn't know at all, Eve thought bitterly.

Eve blew out a breath and dragged a hand through the flowing mane of wayward dark blond hair. She stared at the computer screen on her laptop, silently seeking answers she knew weren't about to materialize. Barring that, she needed a distraction.

My kingdom for a distraction, she thought whimsically.

After shutting down the animal hospital for the night, the animal hospital that had once borne only her father's nameplate across the front door and where she had grown up, surrounded by animals in need of care and a kind, gentle father, Eve had gone home and retreated to her inner office. She'd turned on her computer to do a little research into the condition of the near-blinded dachshund that had been brought in today, searching for a possible way to reverse, or at least halt the condition. Searching, she supposed, for a miracle.

How she'd gotten to a chat room for expectant single moms was almost as mysterious to her as how she'd gotten in this condition in the first place.

Actually more so, she mused.

Of course she knew all about the mechanics of becoming pregnant, but it was how and why she'd gotten to that point that utterly mystified her. In hindsight, it just didn't seem possible.

She knew exactly what she wanted to do with her life, had known ever since she could remember. At least she'd known professionally. She was exactly what she wanted to be: a veterinarian, caring for a host of dogs and cats just the way her father had.

What she wanted for her private life was another matter. Oh, she knew that she wanted to go the traditional route. Wanted a husband and a family. Eventually.

She would have sworn that she hadn't wanted to reverse that order, but apparently she had no choice in the matter now.

Unless, as her sister in Sacramento had urged, she give up the baby.

There was no way Eve wanted to do that. Not because she viewed the little passenger she was carrying around as a love child, the living testimony of the passion that had existed between her and Adam. No, that didn't enter into it at all. The baby, whose due date Eve's ob-gyn had calculated was still a long two weeks away, was an extension of her, a little person whom for reasons that were beyond her, God had seen fit to entrust to her.

She was even looking forward to holding the baby in her arms. But she wasn't looking forward to dealing with being alone at a time when the baby's father's emotional support would have meant so much.

The latter was her own fault, she supposed.

No one had told her to pick up in the middle of the night and flee from Santa Barbara, secretly running back home to Laguna Beach.

"But how couldn't I?" she said aloud.

Tessa, dead to the world only a heartbeat ago, raised her head and looked at Eve with deep brown eyes. The next second, seeing that there was no emergency, Tessa went back to sleep.

Leaning over, Eve ran her hand over the dog's head, struggled to bank down her agitation. Petting her dog usually helped calm her.

But not tonight.

Tonight, the agitation refused to leave, refused to budge.

Maybe it was because tonight was Halloween, she thought. Maybe that was why she couldn't seem to shake the feeling that someone was watching her.

She sighed again.

Adam Smythe had been almost stereotypically handsome, not to mention the last word in "sexy." Added to that he was charming and he had taken her breath away from the very first moment she'd walked into his rare, first-editions bookstore. The moment he had looked her way, she'd felt as if an arrow had been shot straight into her heart.

At the time she'd been looking for a special birthday present for her father. Warren Walters loved everything that had ever come from Mark Twain's pen. What she'd wound up getting, along with a fairly well-preserved first edition of *A Connecticut Yankee in King Arthur's Court,* was a prepackaged heartache.

Oh, Adam hadn't looked like a heartache at first or even at tenth glance. He looked like a drop-dead gorgeous specimen of manhood who, given that this was California, she wouldn't have been surprised if the tall, dark-haired, green-eyed man had said he was just running the bookstore until that big acting break came that would propel him into being the country's next great heartthrob.

To add to this image, Adam was soft-spoken, slightly reserved, and he exuded such a powerful aura of authority that he'd instantly made her feel safe.

Eve laughed now, shaking her head at her incredible naiveté.

Talk about getting the wrong signal.

There had been nothing safe about Adam. He made her lose control in a heartbeat. Some of the boys in high school, and then college, she recalled, had referred to her as the Ice Princess.

"I certainly melted fast enough with him," she told her faithful, sleeping companion. Tessa didn't even stir this time.

One dinner.

One dinner had been all it had taken and she was ready to completely surrender her self-imposed code of ethics and abandon the way she'd behaved for her entire adult life without so much as a backward glance. When Adam had leaned over to brush back a loose strand of hair from her cheek, she turned into a furnace. Raging heat flashed through her limbs. Through her entire body.

And then he'd kissed her.

God, when Adam kissed her, she'd felt as if she were literally having an out-of-body experience.

And suddenly, without warning, Adam had drawn away and she came crashing down to earth like a speeding meteorite. A very confused meteorite.

She was accustomed to men being the aggressors, to having to somehow diplomatically hold them at bay without hurting their feelings or their egos. But this had been the other way around. Adam had been the one who had pulled back. And she had been the one who ultimately pushed.

Very simply, there'd been something about Adam that had turned her inside out. Their night together was the stuff of fantasies.

And then, just like that, all her thoughts centered around him. She couldn't wait until the next time they were together, couldn't wait to hear the sound of his voice, to catch a whiff of the scent that was the combination of his shaving cream mixing with his aftershave.

Adam had become her sun and anytime she wasn't around him, she felt as if she'd been plunged into soul-consuming darkness.

What a crock.

How could she, a heretofore intelligent woman, have been so blind, so dumb?

Smitten teenage girls—very young smitten teenage girls—felt this way, not a woman who practiced veterinarian medicine, who was a responsible, levelheaded and dedicated person.

Except that she had.

Into every paradise, a snake must slither and her paradise was no different. It occurred shortly after the first time—the only time—that they made love.

Made love.

The phrase lingered now in her brain like a haunting refrain.

Even today, knowing what she knew, it was still hard

not to feel the excitement pulsing through her body at the mere memory of those precious, exquisite moments she'd spent lost in Adam's arms, in his embrace. Even though it seemed impossible, he was simultaneously the most gentle, caring, yet passionate lover ever created. And he had been hers.

Looking back, she could honestly say, if only to herself, that they hadn't made love. They had made poetry.

Remembering the moment, Eve felt her body aching for him.

"Stop it," she upbraided herself.

Tessa raised her head, this time quickly, as if she was ready to dart away, afraid that she'd caused her mistress some displeasure. Displeasure that brought punishment with it.

Eve instantly felt guilty. "No, not you, girl," she said in a soothing voice, running her hand over the dog's head and stroking it. "I'm just talking to myself." She looked at the dog and smiled sadly. "Too bad you can't talk, then maybe my thoughts wouldn't keep getting carried away like this."

Calmed, Tessa lowered her head again, resting it on her paws. She was asleep in less than a minute, this time snoring gently.

Eve smiled at her, shaking her head. "I love you the way you are, but I wish you were human."

She craved companionship, someone to communicate with. But her father was gone. He had died less than a month after she'd come back home. Heartbroken, she'd handled all the funeral arrangements. Angela and her family had come down on the day of the funeral and had left by its end. Angela had left a trail of excuses in her wake. Eve didn't blame her. Angela and her family had a life to get back to.

It was several days after her father's funeral, as she wandered around the empty house, looking for a place for herself, that she finally had to admit what she had been trying desperately to ignore. She was pregnant.

At least her father had been spared that, Eve thought, forever trying to look on the bright side of things.

Eve knew he would have been there for her, supporting her—unlike her sister—no matter what her decision regarding the baby's future. But somewhere deep down inside, Eve was fairly certain her father would have felt disappointed. He'd always thought of her as perfect.

Again, she shook her head, her sad smile barely moving the corners of her mouth. "'Fraid not, Dad. So far from perfect, it would boggle your mind."

Just then, she felt a sharp pain. The baby was kicking. Again. It had been restless all day.

Probably tired of its closed quarters, Eve thought. Maybe he or she was claustrophobic, the way she was.

Without thinking, Eve lifted one hand from the keyboard and placed it over the swell of her abdomen, massaging the area that was the origin of the pain this time, even though it did no good.

Was it her imagination, or was she growing bigger and bigger by the hour?

"Won't be long now, baby," she murmured to her stomach.

She had a little more than two weeks to go. Part of her couldn't wait to finally have this all over with, to give birth and meet this little person who had turned her world completely upside down. The other part of her was content to let this state continue. She was terrified of the delivery. Not of what she imagined would be the pain, she'd helped birth enough animals to know exactly what to expect in that respect. No, she was afraid of what lay ahead after the birthing pains had subsided. When the real challenge kicked in.

"You know it's selfish of you to keep it," Angela had told her for the umpteenth time when she'd called last week. There was a knowing air of superiority in her sister's voice. Angela was convinced she *always* knew what was best. "It needs a mother *and* a father. Since you decided to have it, you really should give it up for adoption."

"'It' is a baby," Eve had shot back, one of the few times she'd lost her temper. But she was thoroughly annoyed at the flippant, cavalier way her sister was talking to her. Angela was acting as if she had the inside track on how to live life the right way just because she was married and had the idyllic number of children: two, a boy and a girl. "And what the baby needs is a mother who loves unconditionally."

"Obviously," had been Angela's snide retort. Eve knew that her older sister referred not to her loving the baby, but to the situation that had resulted in the creation of this baby. "Look, why won't you tell the father that he has a responsibility—"

Eve cut her short. "Because I won't, that's all. Subject closed," she'd said firmly.

She wasn't about to tell Angela the reason she wouldn't notify Adam of his paternity. Even under perfect conditions, she wouldn't have wanted the father of her child to feel obligated to "step up and do the right thing," as Angela had declared. When she did get married, it would be because the man who had her heart wanted to marry her, not because he felt he *had* to marry her.

And conditions were far from perfect. She hadn't even told Angela Adam's name, much less what it was that had sent her running back home to get away from the potential heartache that Adam Smythe—if that was even his name—represented.

Eve closed her eyes, remembering that night. She might have even still been in Santa Barbara, running the animal clinic there, if she hadn't overheard Adam on the phone. Closing early for the night, she'd decided to surprise Adam and arrive early for their date. He was on the telephone, his back to her, talking to a potential customer. As she listened, waiting for him to finish, she realized that he wasn't talking to a customer about one of the books in his shop, but someone calling him about obtaining drugs.

Horror filled her as she realized that the man who had lit up her world, who was her baby's father, was one of the lowest life-forms on this earth: a drug dealer.

The bookstore was just a cover.

Her soul twisted in disappointment. She couldn't even bring herself to confront him, to demand to know why he hadn't told her he was immersed in this dark world before they'd gotten involved with one another.

Before she'd fallen in love with him.

She'd felt so sick, so betrayed and so lost. She'd slipped out of the store quickly and silently. Hurrying to her apartment, she'd called him, struggling to hide her anger and hurt, and told Adam that she wasn't feeling well. Sympathetic, he'd offered to come over to keep her company, but she'd turned him down, saying she was afraid she might be contagious. Promising to call him the next day with an update, she'd hung up.

It took her less than an hour to pack.

She'd left Adam a note, telling him she knew what he was involved in and begging him to get out before he became just another dead statistic. And then, after calling the clinic and telling her assistant that there was an emergency and she had to leave, Eve did just that.

All water under the bridge, she told herself now wearily. Can't unring a bell. Adam was what he was— and she was pregnant. She was just going to have to make the best of it.

Right now, that actually involved doing something else she'd never thought she would do: pouring out her heart to a perfect stranger.

But then, that was exactly what made it so safe and cathartic. She was never going to see the stranger she'd found online, never going to meet MysteryMom, the woman who ran the support Web site she'd discovered several weeks ago. At the time, she hadn't thought she would write more than once, but venting, getting it all out, proved to be almost euphoric. And it really did make her feel better to unburden herself like this, cloaked in anonymity. Though she wanted to be, she just couldn't remain tight-lipped right now.

Besides, confession was supposed to be good for the soul, right?

God knew, she hadn't intended on going back to the Web site when she'd sat down tonight, but it had been a long, trying day and after hunting for answers regarding her nearly blind patient, answers that had turned out not to be very optimistic. She'd found herself drawn back to MysteryMom and the woman's easygoing, low-keyed common sense. It was like having a friend, and right now, she could stand to have a friend. A female friend who seemed to know exactly what she was going through.

Once she logged on, all it had taken were a few well-intentioned questions from MysteryMom and suddenly the floodgates had been tapped and Eve found herself typing so fast, there was almost smoke coming from her fingers.

Maybe tomorrow, she'd regret all this, Eve thought philosophically. But then, how could she possibly be in any worse shape than she already was? Wildly in love nine months ago, then wildly disappointed—and now, wildly pregnant.

Hell of a journey, she thought, typing words to that effect to the sympathetic MysteryMom.

And then Eve stopped, leaning back in her chair. She glanced toward her sleeping shadow. "I just hope that 'MysteryMom' isn't some cigar chomping, hairy-knuckled oaf getting his jollies by pretending to be a sympathetic single mom," she said to Tessa.

Tessa merely yawned and went back to sleeping.

Eve was about to type another thought when she heard the doorbell ring.

More trick or treaters.

With a sigh, Eve gripped the arms on her chair and pushed herself up.

She missed being able to spring to her feet, but she supposed it could be worse. At least she could still see her feet. When Angela had been pregnant with her first child, Renee, she couldn't see her feet after entering her seventh month.

Tessa was on all four of hers, padding quietly behind her, a four-legged, furry shadow determined to remain close.

Eve passed a mirror on her way to the front door. "At least I don't look like a blimp," she consoled herself.

A goblin, a fairy princess and what looked like a robot, none of whom could have been over ten, shouted "Trick or treat!" at her the moment she opened the door. Delighted, Eve grabbed a handful of candy from the bowl she had placed by the front door and divided the candy between them.

The goblin paused, relishing his booty, and obviously staring at her. "What are you supposed to be?"

Eve didn't even hesitate. "A pumpkin." It sounded better to her than "beached whale."

"But you're not orange," the robot protested.

Eve snapped her fingers. "Knew I forgot something. Thanks for letting me know."

Only the fairy princess said nothing beyond, "Thank you," looking at her knowingly, as if, even at that age, there was an unconscious bond that existed within the female gender.

And then her little visitors ran off, laughing, all beneath the distant, watchful scrutiny of one of their parents.

As she slowly closed her front door, Eve realized that the feeling was back. The one that whispered there was someone out there, watching her. Hoping to either catch him or her, or render a death knell to the unnerving feeling, she swung open her door again and looked around.

Nothing.

Again.

She frowned, closing the door all the way this time. The excitement over, Tessa turned away from the door. "If there is someone out there, promise you'll rip them limb from limb if they try to break in, Tessa."

The dog gave no indication that she heard any of the request. Instead, she trotted back to the office and reclaimed her position beneath the desk.

"I feel so safe now," Eve murmured to the dog as she lowered herself into the office chair again and once more immersed herself in the comforting words of MysteryMom. It wasn't that she was a believer in the old saying that misery loved company. It was just that knowing someone else had gone through what she was going through and survived made her feel more heartened.

It was something to cling to.

Chapter 2

After more than two years undercover, disappearing into the shadows had become second nature to Adam Serrano.

Usually the object of his surveillance was an unsavory character involved in the ever-mushrooming, lethal drug trade, not a female veterinarian with killer legs, liquid blue eyes and a soul Snow White would have been in awe of.

The anonymous tip that had appeared without warning on his computer yesterday morning had been right. Eve Walters was right here in Laguna Beach, practically right under his nose.

Who would have thought it?

The irony of the situation was still very fresh in his mind. She had disappeared on him eight months ago, doing what he hadn't been able to bring himself to do: leaving. Reading her letter, a letter he still had in his possession, had cut small, jagged holes in his soul. His first instinct had been to go after her, to find her and bring her back.

But he'd forced himself to refrain.

It hadn't been easy. Eventually, his common sense had prevailed. This was for the best.

Though he missed Eve more than he would have ever thought possible, Adam had every intention of allowing her to stay out of his life. Being part of his life would have been far too dangerous for her.

The nature of his "business," searching for the source of the latest flood of heroin, had brought him here, down to southern California. These days, the hard reality of it was that, despite his agency's efforts, the drug culture was alive and thriving absolutely everywhere. The drugs on the street apparently knew no caste system, bringing down the rich, as well as the poor. The only difference was that the rich didn't need to knock over a liquor store, or rob an elderly couple or kill some unsuspecting innocent to feed their habit. That's what Mommy and Daddy were for, blindly throwing money at the problem instead of helping their spoiled, pampered offspring morph into respectable people.

Life didn't work that way. But it was obviously still full of surprises.

Not the least of which was that his work had brought him down here, almost at Eve's door, as it were.

But moving the base of his "operation" to Laguna still wouldn't have had him skulking around, camping out in unmarked cars and hiding in doorways to catch a glimpse of her or acting like some wayward guardian angel if that anonymous message on his computer hadn't knocked him for a loop.

"Eve is pregnant with your baby." The terse sentence was followed by an address. Nothing more.

He'd presumed the address belonged to Eve. Minimal effort via his computer had proven him right. He recalled her mentioning that she had grown up somewhere in this area and that her dad had had an animal hospital here.

When he looked up the animal hospitals in and around Laguna, he found an "E. Walters" listed. He remembered her telling him that her father's name was Warren. That meant that she was now running the Animal Hospital of Laguna Beach.

And she was pregnant, supposedly with his baby.

Even so, Adam had debated ignoring the message, telling himself it was some kind of trick to have him come forward. And even if it wasn't a trick, he could do nothing about the situation. It was her body, not his. Whether or not she kept this baby was up to her, not him.

That argument had lasted all of ten minutes, if that long. Even as he posed it, Adam knew he had to see for himself whether or not it was true.

He fervently hoped that it wasn't.

But it was. Or, at least, she was carrying someone's child.

In his gut, he knew it was his.

Juggling things so that he could put everything else temporarily on hold for the evening, Adam stationed himself in a nondescript vehicle on the through street that ran by Eve's house. He was careful to park on the opposite side, waiting to catch another glimpse of the only woman who had managed to break through his carefully constructed barriers.

It was Halloween and he knew the way Eve felt about kids. The same way she felt about helpless animals. No way was she going to be one of those people who either left their home for the evening every Halloween or pretended not to hear the doorbell or the noise generated by approaching bands of costumed children.

Personally, he never liked the holiday. Dealing with the scum of the earth for the last ten years, he knew what was out there. And what could happen to trusting children.

Hell, if he had a kid...

He *did* have a kid, Adam realized abruptly. Or would have one. Soon, if his math served him.

Damn, he hadn't gotten used to that idea yet.

A father.

Him.

Maybe the baby wasn't his, Adam thought. A woman as beautiful as Eve Walters had to have a lot of men after her. A lot of men trying to get her to sleep with them...

Even as he made the excuses, Adam knew they weren't true. Eve wasn't the type to sleep around. He'd known that even before they'd made love. And when they had, he'd discovered to his everlasting surprise that she was a virgin. He'd been her first.

How?

How the hell had this happened? he silently demanded. He'd made sure he used protection. Pausing in the middle of heated passion had been damn awkward, but he had done it, mindful of the consequences if he didn't. Even so, she had made him lose his head and it had been all he could do to hold on to his common sense.

Common sense, now there was a misnomer. Common sense just wasn't common. If he'd actually had any, he would've gotten a grip on himself then and there. Instead of reaching for a condom, he would have reached for his jeans and walked away.

Adam shook his head. Who the hell was he kidding? A saint couldn't have walked away from Eve, not when things had reached that level. Not with that delicious mouth of hers. Not with that body, slick with sweat and desire, his for the taking. And God knew he wasn't a saint—far from it. He was just a man. And she had made him vulnerable.

And now, apparently, he had returned the favor and done the same to her.

He had no family, not anymore. And when it was only him, the danger didn't matter.

But now it mattered.

If she was pregnant, he was going to need to protect her. If these rich lowlifes he dealt with found out she was pregnant with his baby, there was more than a slim chance, if things went awry, that they would do something to her. He put nothing past them, nothing past the middle man he was currently working with, a college senior majoring in heroin distribution. Danny Sederholm might kidnap Eve—or the baby— if it gave the kid the advantage and secured leverage against him. Nobody trusted anybody in this so-called "business."

Adam shifted in his seat, feeling restless and confined. Where were the hoards of kids, wandering around the neighborhood and ringing doorbells in their quest for cavities? Had they all suddenly come to their senses and abandoned the trick-or-treating ritual?

Get a grip, Serrano.

He wasn't usually this impatient. But this was different. This wasn't just about him.

Hell, he would have felt a lot better just knowing who the message had come from.

The fact that it could all be a trap was not lost on him. No computer novice, he'd spent a good part of yesterday trying to trace where the message had originated. A good part of yesterday was spent in frustration.

Striking out, he'd gotten in contact with his handler, Hugh Patterson, who in turn had turned Spenser onto the task. Spenser was a wunderkind when it came to the computer. When Spenser failed to find where the e-mail had come from, he knew that they were dealing with a five-star pro.

Good pro or bad pro?

Adam hadn't the slightest idea, but for now, his anonymous tipster didn't seem to have an agenda, other than passing on this tidbit of information. Why he or she had done that, Adam hadn't a clue. Was it to taunt him, to show him he was vulnerable, or to get him to stand up and do the right thing? Or was this tipster just out to entertain himself or play deus ex machina behind the scenes?

Adam wished he knew.

But he did know what his next step had to be. And he took it.

Laura Delaney sat down at her desk, getting back to her Web site. Jeremy was finally in bed, asleep, or at least, asleep for the time being. She had no doubt that at least some of the candy he'd collected tonight had found its way into his bottomless tummy despite her strict rules about his only eating two pieces tonight and evenly doling out the rest for the following week. She'd offered those terms, hoping that a compromise would be reached at five. Maybe six.

Bid low, go high, she thought, amused.

She loved this holiday, loved seeing the excitement in her young son's eyes. Taking after her, Jeremy had started planning his costume right after school began in September. Most of all, she loved seeing life through his deep brown eyes. Everything felt so fresh, so new again seeing it from Jeremy's perspective. After all the time she'd spent in the CIA, this new outlook was a godsend to her.

Getting pregnant with Jeremy was definitely the best thing that had ever happened to her.

Although it certainly hadn't felt so at the time.

At the time, making the discovery a week after her intense debriefing in Singapore, the pregnancy had knocked the pins right out from beneath her world. And there was never any question as to who the father was. Jeremy's father was a dynamic, larger-than-life handsome man who had quite literally saved her life.

The whole thing had been almost like a scene out of

the movies. The one where the hero put out his hand to the heroine and growled darkly, "Come with me if you want to live."

She'd wanted to live all right. Pinned down in a hopeless situation, knowing she'd be dead by dawn if she stayed, she'd had no recourse but to come with the man who had suddenly burst into her life.

In true knight-in-shining-armor style, he'd used his body to shield hers and had hustled her out of what would have been a terminal situation. A hairbreadth away from being captured by the people she, as a CIA operative, had been sent to spy on, Laura had had no illusions about her situation. Had he not suddenly materialized in that embassy room, seemingly out of nowhere, she knew she would not have lived to see another sunrise.

Instead, she'd lived to watch the sunrise in a small fishing hut, sequestered in his arms. Funny how almost dying makes you so anxious to live, to experience and savor everything. The escape, the pursuit and then hiding in a fishing village, posing as fishermen, had all contributed to her heightened desire to live. Her desire to seize all that life had to offer.

What life had offered was a man whose name she never learned.

She had learned that she hadn't been afraid to seize the moment, and neither had he. They were drawn to one another like the missing two halves of a whole. Their coming together was nothing short of earthshaking. It had been predestined.

Then came the dawn and the rest of life.

He smuggled her out of the village, put her on a

transport plane and then, much too quickly, faded out of her life. Faded even though she asked more than one operative who the masked man was. Time and again, she received conflicting answers. The upshot was that no one seemed to know who he was or where he came from. It was almost as if he was a phantom.

Laura went on asking more urgently when she discovered that she was pregnant. But the result remained the same. No one could tell her. The few leads she had all ended in a dead end, taking her to operatives who turned out not to be the man who had saved her life and planted another inside her.

Pregnant, she had another life to think about other than her own. Laura decided she had no choice but to leave her present life behind. Because of her love of animals and having been raised on a ranch, she took up horse training in an effort to create a stable—no pun intended—normal life for her son.

These days, the life she'd once led almost seemed like a dream, or an action novel she'd read a long, long time ago. The only thing left to remind her that she had once actually been a CIA operative was her ability to utilize information—and sources—to allow her to find people. Ironically, despite numerous tries, she couldn't find Jeremy's father, but once she'd read Eve Walters's e-mail and learned the woman's story, she had used all the information available to her to see if she could track down the so-called "drug dealer" who had impregnated the woman.

As she read Eve's story, her gut almost immediately told her that the man who had fathered Eve's baby wasn't the drug pusher the woman believed him to be.

Laura knew the life, knew the deceptions that were so necessary in order to maintain a cover. Something she couldn't put into words told her that Eve's "Adam" was part of some kind of government agency.

A little research and calling in several favors from old friends proved her right.

Adam Smythe was actually Adam Serrano, a DEA agent who had been working undercover for the last two years. There was more background on the man, but that was all she was interested in. Laura saw no reason to delve into the man's history any further than was absolutely necessary. The life she led now made her acutely aware of the need for, and seductive appeal of, privacy. She gave Adam Serrano his.

Armed with this information, it took little for her to find both Adam's Internet server and with that, his e-mail address. Her stark e-mail message to him went out the moment she secured it.

If Adam was anything like her, she reasoned, his sense of family would leap to the foreground, especially since he had none. She was fairly certain that he would lose no time trying to track down the mother of this unborn child he hadn't realized was in the offing.

Laura was more than a little tempted to e-mail Eve and let her know that Adam was coming, but that might have made the woman bolt. Bolting was the last thing she needed to do at this late stage in her pregnancy.

Eve needed exactly what she was most likely going to get.

What she, herself, would have loved to get, Laura thought wistfully.

But, except for an occasional daydream, she had

given up the fantasy that had her mystery man knocking on her door, the way she envisioned Adam doing now, or definitely in the very near future, on Eve's door.

Laura smiled as she replayed the thought. It wasn't every day a girl got the chance to bring Adam and Eve together, she mused, more than a little pleased with herself.

With renewed purpose, Laura went on to read the next e-mail that had been sent to her site from another single mom.

The doorbell was ringing.

Eve pressed her lips together. She had just shut down her computer for the night. Glancing at her watch, she saw that it was almost nine o'clock.

Nine o'clock and she was struggling to keep her eyes open.

Some party girl she was, Eve mocked herself. She could remember going two days without sleep when she was in college. Three days once, she recalled. There was no way she could do that now. But then, this pregnancy and the tension that had come with it served to drain her and make her overly tired more than she cared to acknowledge.

This was probably nothing compared to how tired she was going to be once the baby learned how to walk and get into things, she thought. She was looking forward to that, she realized. Looking forward to being a parent—

The doorbell rang again.

What kind of a responsible parent allowed their child to still be out, trick-or-treating at this hour? The little ones needed to be home, asleep in their beds, or at least in their beds.

Most likely it was another one of those high school kids, she thought, bracing her hands on the chair's armrests and pushing herself to her feet. She'd had several of those tonight, costumed kids who towered over her. One looked old enough to shave.

She hated the way they abused Halloween, horning in on a holiday that was intended for little children to enjoy. Oh, well, she still had some candy left over. She might as well give it to them. It was better for her that way.

Eve knew her weakness. If there was candy hanging around in a bowl, no matter what she promised herself about being good, the pieces would eventually find their way into her mouth. The problem was, Eve thought, she had never met a piece of candy, chocolate or otherwise she didn't like.

"Time to get rid of the temptation," she told Tessa. Gently snoring, the dog ignored her.

Picking up the bowl, Eve carried it with her as she made her way to the front door.

"Some guard dog you are," she quipped, tossing the remark over her shoulder. Tessa still didn't stir.

About to open the door, she had to stop for a second as yet another pain seized her, stealing her breath and causing her to all but double over. This was getting very old. Just as perspiration broke out all along her brow, the pain receded. She let out a long breath and then reached for the front door.

Since she was right-handed, Eve had to shift the bowl over to her left side and then open the door with her right.

But this time, no chorus of "Trick or treat!"—even a baritone chorus—greeted her.

Instead, the uncostumed, tall, dark and still pulse-racingly handsome man who was standing on her doorstep said, "Hello, Eve."

The lights in the living room behind her seemed to dim slightly, even as her head began to spin about. Eve struggled to catch hold of it. Reality and everything that went with it distanced itself from her.

The bowl she was holding slipped out of her hand and onto the light gray tiled floor, shattering the second it made contact.

It was only by sheer luck that she hadn't gone down with it.

Chapter 3

Adam. Here.

How?

Stunned, the first coherent thought that shot through Eve's mind was to somehow cover up the rounded expanse of her belly so that Adam wouldn't notice that she was pregnant.

But it was far too late for that.

Those emerald-green eyes of his that she'd once loved so much slid down, taking in the swell of his child.

Her mouth felt as dry as cotton as she struggled to access her brain. The organ became temporarily paralyzed by the sight of the man whose very touch had once been able to move the earth beneath her feet.

Then, as she watched, to her utter amazement Adam

dropped down to his knees right in front of her. For just the tiniest fraction of a second, she thought he was going apologize profusely, swearing by everything he held dear that he'd completely reformed and had been frantically searching for her these last eight months. She knew it was just a hopeless fantasy on her part. Adam would never beg for any reason. It would have been completely out of character for him.

As out of character as a supposed scholar dealing in drugs to provide himself with a lucrative sideline, she thought with no small touch of sarcasm.

As her mind came back into sync, it still took Eve more than a moment to draw in enough air to form any words.

"What—what are you doing here?" she finally managed to ask, addressing the question to the top of his thick, black hair.

"Right now, picking up a bunch of broken glass and several tiny bags of Halloween candy," Adam answered. The bowl had smashed into almost a dozen pieces, too many for him to hold in his hand at one time. Looking up, he asked her, "Do you have a bag or something that I can put this mess into?"

The question sounded so casual, so natural, as if they had never been apart. As if this was just another evening in their lives, following scores of other evenings exactly like it.

But it wasn't just another evening, and they *had* been apart. Moreover, if she'd been successful in her escape from Santa Barbara, they would have remained that way forever.

Despite everything, just looking at him intensified

the longing she'd struggled against almost daily. Eve vaguely remembered a lyric she'd once heard, part of a song whose title she'd long since forgotten. *Leaving him was a lot easier than staying away.*

Truer words were never uttered.

Seeing Adam now, Eve wanted to throw herself into his arms. To hide there, in the shelter of his embrace. In effect, she wanted to hide from the man she'd discovered Adam to be by seeking refuge in the arms of the man she'd thought Adam was.

How crazy was that?

Very.

Her head hurt and her heart ached.

"Or," Adam went on when she continued to stand there, making no reply, "I could just go get it myself if you tell me where you keep your bags."

She needed to regroup, to stop feeling as if she was on the verge of hyperventilating and tell him in no uncertain terms that he had to leave.

The words wouldn't come.

Buying herself some time, struggling against yet another wave of pain emanating from her belly, Eve turned on her heel and went to the kitchen. She braced her hand on the counter and opened the bottom drawer situated just to the right of the sink. It was stuffed with plastic grocery bags waiting to be pressed into service. After taking one out, she made her way back to the front door and prayed she was hallucinating.

She hadn't imagined it.

Adam was still there, crouching with his hands full of broken glass, watching her. Waiting for her to come back.

Adam's very presence mocked the notions that had filled her head such a short time ago. Notions that comprised the happily-ever-after scenario she'd once woven for herself, thinking that *finally* she'd found that one special someone she wanted to face forever with.

Until there was Adam, she'd never been in love before, never even experienced a serious crush. At twenty-nine, she'd begun to think that she was destined to face life alone. But then she'd walked into the secondhand bookstore and lost her heart. Just like that.

She'd even joked with her father when she saw him shortly thereafter, gifting him with the first edition Mark Twain book she'd bought in Adam's store, that she'd never believed love at first sight was anything but a myth—until she'd fallen victim to it.

Victim.

Now there was a good word. Because she really was the victim here. She and this baby. A victim of her own stupidity and her far-too-trusting nature. Otherwise, maybe she would have noticed some things that were awry, things that she should have scrutinized more closely. Warning signs. They had to have been there if she hadn't been so blind, so willing to love.

She bit back a sigh. She wasn't up to this. Wasn't up to dealing with seeing Adam, especially not now, when she felt as sluggish as an elephant that had been hit with a giant tranquilizer dart.

Eve held out the plastic grocery bag. Adam took it from her, murmuring "Thanks," and smiling that lopsided, sensual smile of his she discovered she still wasn't immune to.

She stood there, trying not to think, not to feel, as

Adam gathered up the last of the glass and disposed of it in the bag.

Just then, as if suddenly hearing the sound of his voice, Tessa came charging out of the office to investigate. Seeing him, she immediately dashed toward Adam, wagging her tail like a metronome that had been set at triple time.

"Hi, Tessa," Adam said with a laugh, petting the excited dog and trying not to let her knock him over. "How've you been, girl?"

In response, Tessa licked his face.

So much for allies, Eve thought.

Still petting the dog, Adam looked at her. "I think I got it all," he told Eve. "But to be on the safe side, I'd suggest you vacuum the area." Standing up, taking care not to let the excited dog overwhelm him, he decided to augment his statement. "Better yet, tell me where you keep your vacuum cleaner and I'll vacuum the area for you." Anticipating an argument, Adam added, "It's the least I can do—seeing as how the sight of me made you drop the bowl in the first place."

Eve squared her shoulders. *Don't let him get to you, damn it. Don't!*

"I can do my own vacuuming," she told him in a voice that had a slight tremor in it.

He eyed her dubiously, his smile fading and becoming a thing of the past. "You sure? Pushing something heavy around like that might cause you to go into labor prematurely."

She wanted him out of here—before she wound up caving. "Did you get a medical degree since I last saw you?"

His eyes remained on hers. It took everything she had not to let them get to her. Not to just give up and hold on to him the way she couldn't seem to hold on to her anger.

"A lot of things happened since I last saw you," he told her, his voice low, "but my getting a medical degree wasn't among them."

It was the same tone that used to ripple along her skin, exciting her. Well, it didn't excite her anymore. *It didn't,* she fiercely insisted.

"I'm just passing on some common sense," Adam concluded.

She did her best to make him leave. "Always a first time," she answered sarcastically.

Adam waited for her to continue venting. When she didn't, he raised an eyebrow.

"That's it?" he asked. "Nothing more? No more slings and arrows and hot words?" He knew it was baiting her, but the way he saw it, she deserved to be able to yell at him, to put her anger into words. God knew she had the right.

But she just looked at him, the light leaving her eyes. That hurt him more than anything she could have said, because he knew that he'd done that to her.

"What's the point?" she countered sadly, half lifting her shoulders in a careless shrug.

"The point is that it might make you feel better," Adam told her. "It might help restore some equilibrium in your world."

She was a long way from having that happen, she thought. A *long* way. "The only thing that would do either would be if I'd never met you."

He had that coming and he knew it. He regretted

their time together only because it had placed her in jeopardy and it ultimately had hurt her. That had never been his intention.

In an absolute, personal sense, he'd never, not even for a moment, regretted having her in his life, no matter how short the time they had together had been. But, even though she didn't know it, she'd had her revenge. Eve had upended his world, showing him everything he'd given up to do what he did, to be what he was. She'd showed him everything he could have had if his life had gone differently.

At least he had a life, he reminded himself.

Which was more than Mona had.

Mona, his kid sister, had been bright, beautiful and blessed with the ability to light up a room the moment she entered it. Her family and friends were all certain that she could have had the world at her feet just by wishing it.

Instead, she opted to keep it at bay, losing herself in the dark, forbidding haze of heroin and meth until no one who loved her could even recognize her. Despite his alternating between pleading with her and railing at her, his sister had continued using even as she made him promise after promise to stop.

When she finally did stop, it hadn't been voluntarily. He'd found her lying facedown on the floor of the apartment he'd been paying for, a victim of a drug overdose. No frantic attempts at CPR on his part could revive her. His sister was gone, another statistic in the increasingly unsuccessful war on drugs. His crusade against drugs began that morning.

And the way he viewed it, it hadn't cost him anything. Until he'd met Eve.

"Where do you keep the vacuum cleaner?" he repeated, his voice a little gruffer.

"I said I'd take care of it," Eve insisted, holding her ground.

He let her win. Maybe she needed that. With a shrug, Adam bent down to pick up the spilled candy. Cradling the small bags, bars and boxes against his chest, he rose to his feet again.

"Where do you want me to put these?"

The answer flashed through her head, but it wasn't her way to say things like that, no matter how tempted she was or how warranted her flippant remark might have actually been. Adam might not have any honor left, but she still did.

Was that why she was carrying the drug dealer's baby? a taunting voice in her head mocked.

"Over there will be fine," she told him, nodding toward the coffee table.

Adam crossed over to it and let the candy rain down from his arms onto the table.

His back was to her. An image flashed through her brain. The way his back had looked as he moved to leave his bed after they'd made love. She felt her stomach tightening.

She had to stop that, stop torturing herself. He wasn't the answer to a prayer, he was the personification of a nightmare.

A nightmare in pleasing form.

Eve passed her tongue along her lips, trying to moisten them. They were so dry, they were almost sticking together.

"Why did you come?" she forced herself to ask, making it sound like an accusation.

He turned from the table and looked at her. Had she always looked so delicate? he wondered. "I heard you were pregnant—"

Eve widened her eyes. They had no friends in common and their worlds certainly didn't overlap.

"How did you hear?" she demanded. He just looked at her. "Who told you?" she pressed.

He waved her question away. "Doesn't matter. But I came to see for myself."

She drew herself up to her full five-foot-four height, then spread her arms, giving him an unobstructed view. After a minute, she dropped her arms again. "All right, you saw. Now please leave."

Adam remained where he stood, making no move to do anything of the kind. Tessa was nuzzling his leg and he stroked her head as he took a breath, fortifying himself.

"Is it mine?" he asked.

"No." The denial automatically rose to her lips and shot like a bullet through the air, primed by a she-bear's instincts to protect her unborn cub.

He didn't believe her even though part of him would have really wanted to. It would have made everything so much simpler. It would have taken away not just his sense of guilt, but of responsibility, too. Not to mention that he wouldn't need to feel obligated to protect the baby or her if she wasn't bearing his child.

The hell you wouldn't.

The other part of him fiercely rejected even the suggestion that the seed growing in her belly had come from anyone but him. Even if he never saw Eve again—

and until that anonymous e-mail had turned up on his computer he never planned to—Eve was his soul mate in every sense of the word. He knew that no matter how many women he came across, how many he took to his bed, this one would stand out. This one would always mean more to him than all the others combined.

And he knew her well enough to know that the child was his no matter what she said to the contrary.

"I don't believe you," he told her quietly.

Panic began to form within her. Why had he shown up? Why couldn't he just let her go? And more importantly, why did the sight of him make her yearn like this? She weighed a ton, for God's sake. Women who weighed a ton weren't supposed to suddenly want to have their bones jumped, especially not by someone they knew dwelled with the dregs of society.

Eve did her best to sound distant. "I don't care what you believe," she told him coldly. Tossing her hair over her shoulder, she ordered, "Now go, get out of here. I never want to see you again."

This was where he should retreat. She'd given him the perfect out. He'd come, he'd seen for himself that Eve was pregnant, now it was time to go. He was still undercover and the stakes were now larger than ever. The person he was after was the main player, the head of the drug cartel. The center of the drug trafficking that was filling the local colleges with heroin.

He couldn't jeopardize that. Eve had made it perfectly clear that she didn't want him around. And she'd heatedly denied that he was the father. That meant that he could walk away with a clear conscience.

But he couldn't leave.

It didn't matter what he wished, the fact remained that Eve had been with him a little less than nine months ago. With him in every sense of the word. He knew in his gut the baby was his. If he could do the math, someone else in the organization would do the same. The time to back away, to pretend she'd never been part of his life, was over. Eve and her unborn child were at risk. They needed his protection. He was *not* about to have them on his conscience.

He frowned, then calmly told her, "The calendar doesn't back up what you just said."

"Then get a new calendar," she retorted. "This is *not* your baby." Her voice rose in anger. "Don't you understand? I don't want anything from you. You're free to walk away. So walk," she ordered.

Instead of leaving, he pushed the door closed. The *click* echoed in her head. Nerves rose to the surface even as she struggled to at least look calm.

"Is this why you left?" he asked, his eyes indicating her swollen abdomen. "Because you found out you were pregnant?"

She took offense, although she didn't even know why. Her hormones raged, playing tug-of-war with her emotions.

"No," she retorted hotly, "I left because I found out that you were a drug dealer."

He needed for her to be safe. Needed to watch over her. He knew that he couldn't just post himself on her block indefinitely. This was the kind of neighborhood where an unknown car would attract attention if it was seen lingering for more than a few minutes—and that would inevitably result in a call to the police.

The last thing he wanted was to get involved with the local law enforcement agency, at least not until he could bring down the leader of this little high-class operation. Otherwise, he and a lot of other people would find themselves throwing away two years on a failed mission. And another drug lord would find himself with a free pass.

He owed it to Mona not to let that happen.

In order to do what he needed to do, he knew he needed to lie.

To Eve.

Again.

"Then you'll be happy to know," he told her, "that I'm not part of that world any longer." His eyes held hers and he hated himself for what he was doing, but at the same time, he knew he had to. "I'm just a simple used book dealer."

For just a moment, Eve's heart leaped up in celebration. She was ready to seize the information and clutch it to her chest like an eternal promise. But he had lied to her before—who knows how many times—and once that sort of thing happened, trust was badly splintered if not shattered. Rebuilding the fragile emotion was not the easiest thing in the world.

"How do I know you're not just lying?" she challenged, praying he had an answer that would somehow satisfy her.

"You don't," he admitted simply, surprising her. "You're just going to have to trust me."

And that, Eve thought, was the problem in a nutshell. More than anything in the world, she wanted to believe him. But at the same time, she knew that she just couldn't. Not yet. Not until he proved himself to her and gave her a concrete reason to believe him.

Just then, she thought she felt the baby begin to kick her again. Kick her harder than it had ever kicked before.

Caught off guard, immersed in this new drama, Eve gasped as tears welled up in her eyes.

Sensing both her mistress's anxiety and her pain, Tessa began to pace nervously about before her as Eve clutched at her belly.

Adam reacted immediately. His arms closed around Eve as if he was afraid that she was about to sink down to the floor.

"What's wrong?" he demanded, concern weaving itself through his voice. His eyes searched her face. "What can I do to help?"

Just hold me, Adam, the little voice in her soul whispered to him. *Just hold me and make everything all better again.*

Chapter 4

He didn't like the way she'd suddenly stiffened against him or the fact that her breathing began to sound labored. Why wasn't she answering him?

As he held Eve at arm's length to get a look at her face, he found nothing to reassure him. She was in physical pain.

"Talk to me, Eve. What's wrong?"

"Nothing," she managed to get out, fervently hoping that if she said it with enough conviction, it would be true. But it wasn't. The pain just got more intense. Why wouldn't it stop? "The baby kicked. He's been doing a lot of that today."

"He?" Adam echoed. If he hadn't known better, he would have said that something akin to pride stirred within him. "It's a boy?"

Trying to get behind the pain, or beyond it, Eve hardly heard him. "Yes." Belatedly, she realized what he'd asked her. "Unless it's a girl."

The only reason he felt a tinge of disappointment was because he liked knowing about things ahead of time. It always helped to be prepared. As for the possibility that he might have a daughter instead of a son, he found himself rather liking the idea. If she took after her mother, she'd be a force to be reckoned with.

"Then you don't know?" he concluded.

"No." He was still holding on to her shoulders and she shrugged his hands away. She'd decided to have her baby the old-fashioned way—that included not knowing its sex. "But then, I don't know a lot of things." She eyed him pointedly. "And contrary to the popular belief, ignorance is *not* bliss. It's setting yourself up for a fall."

She hit her intended target with that one. "I never meant to hurt you, Eve," he told her sincerely. "I swear I didn't."

She could almost believe him. But then, Eve thought ruefully, struggling to hold the hot pain burning in her belly at bay, she'd believed him before and look how that had turned out for her.

"You know what they say about the path to hell," she said in a pseudocheerful voice. "It's paved with good intentions."

Adam knew he could just walk away, that it might be better all around if he did, but the look in her eyes—a look he was fairly sure she wasn't even aware of—just wouldn't let him do it. She needed him.

"Look, I know you probably hate me—"

She shook her head, stopping him before he went on.

"I don't hate you, Adam. Hate's a very powerful emotion. I don't feel anything at all for you."

Her eyes were steely as she tried to convince him nothing remained between them but this child waiting to be born. She sincerely doubted if she'd succeeded because she hadn't even been able to convince herself.

She was lying. He *knew* she was lying. One look into her eyes told him that.

Or was he seeing things he wanted to see?

He wasn't the kind of man she deserved, the kind of man she had a right to expect. A nine-to-five kind of guy who left his work behind once he walked out of the office. His "job" was with him 24/7, even when he wasn't undercover and so much more so when he was. Eve deserved infinitely more than just half a man.

But that didn't change the fact that right now, when she was at her most vulnerable, he needed to look out for her. Needed to be her hidden guardian angel.

Damn, he should have never gotten involved with her, never given in to that overwhelming yearning that had stirred so urgently inside of him every time she walked into his store, into his carefully crafted make-believe life.

Up until that time, it had been easy. He'd been so focused on his job, on the target that Hugh, his handler, had turned him on to that he'd been able to successfully resist the women who crossed his path. Even the ones who had been very determined to extend their acquaintance beyond customer and seller.

But then *she* had walked into his store and everything changed.

It'd been raining that morning, an unexpected, quick

shower that had ushered her into the store along with a sheet of rain. Even soaking wet, her hair plastered to her head, Eve had been possibly the most beautiful woman he had ever seen.

He'd found himself talking to her for the better part of an hour, showing her rare edition after rare edition. Giving her a little capsulated history behind each book. He made it a point never to enter a situation without studying it seven ways from sundown and, in this case, he was supposed to be the scholarly owner of a small shop that dealt only with rare books. Consequently, he had a lot of miscellaneous information crammed into his head.

She'd appeared to hang on every word.

It had been the best time of his life and he wished he could recapture it. But he couldn't.

"All right," Adam said evenly, "you don't feel anything at all for me. I'm not asking you to, but I want you to know that I'm going to be here for you if you need me."

"Won't that be a killer commute for you?" she asked cynically. "Driving from here to Santa Barbara and back every day?"

"I won't be commuting that far."

She didn't understand, but was in too much pain to get the whole story. She blinked hard, clenching her fists at her sides as if that could somehow chase it away. "What about your bookstore?"

"I relocated it," he told her simply, then added an expedient lie. "I lost my lease and Laguna Beach seemed like a nice setting for the shop."

Before she'd discovered his dual life, she would have been thrilled with the idea that Adam had relocated to be close to her, that he had gone searching for her when she'd disappeared and once he'd found where she had gone, he'd rearranged his life just to be nearby.

But those kind of thoughts belonged to a naive, innocent young woman. She was no longer that, no longer naive. Or innocent. And the fault for that partially lay with him.

She needed to discourage him, to make him leave her alone—before she became too weak to follow through. "I don't need you to be 'here' for me, Adam. I've moved on. I'm seeing someone," she informed him tersely.

A sharp pain flared in his gut. He'd lost her. Before he'd ever really had her.

Schooled in not showing emotion, his expression remained unchanged. "Is it serious?"

The lies didn't get easier, but she had no choice. She needed to protect her baby at all costs, and that meant protecting the child from its father.

"Yes. Very. Josiah wants to adopt the baby." Silently, she apologized to Josiah Turner, but the seventy-year-old man's name was the first one to pop into her head. The man was like an uncle to her. She'd known him all her life, from the time she would frequent her father's animal clinic. Whenever he wasn't away on business, Josiah would bring his dogs to her father for routine care. And when he was away, he would board them at the clinic.

When her father died shortly after her return, the retired widower had arbitrarily appointed himself her guardian angel, determined to protect her, especially when it became apparent that she was pregnant.

"Good for you," Adam said, doing his best to infuse an upbeat note into his voice. He still intended to watch over her, but at least she wasn't going to be alone. This meant that he could maintain vigil from a distance. And if knowing that someone else would be holding her, making love with her, stuck a hot knife into his gut, well, that was his problem, not hers. "Then I'll be going."

But even as he told her, his feet didn't seem to want to move. Stalling for time until he could get himself to go, Adam took out one of the business cards he'd had printed just last week and held it out to her.

"In case you ever want to find another first edition," he explained.

When she made no effort to take it from him, he took her hand in his and placed the card with the new bookstore's address and phone number into her palm, closing her fingers over it.

The next moment, as he began to withdraw his hand, she suddenly grabbed his wrist and squeezed it. Hard.

She looked as startled as he was. Adam searched her face. "Eve?"

This time, she made no answer. Instead, Adam watched the color completely drain out of her face and heard her catch her breath the way someone did when they didn't want to scream.

It didn't take much for him to put two and two together. "It's time, isn't it?"

Her eyes were wide as she slanted them toward his. "No, no, it's not. It's not time," she insisted heatedly. "I'm not supposed to be due for another three weeks. Maybe four." Even as she said it, another wave of pain engulfed her. "Oh, God."

Still clutching his wrist, she almost buckled right in

front of him. Adam quickly put his arm around her shoulders. Drawing her to him, he held her up.

"Looks like the baby doesn't have a calendar in there," he told her.

"I'll be all right," she said fiercely, more to reassure herself than him. She glanced toward the living room. "I just need to sit down."

But when she tried to cross to the sofa, he continued to hold her against him. "You might need to sit down, but you're not going to be all right," he told her. She was about to protest again when Adam nodded at the floor directly beneath her feet. She followed his line of vision. The small pool made his argument for him. "Your water just broke."

"No," she cried in vain denial.

There was no time to go back and forth about this. She was in labor. "I'll drive you to the hospital," he told her firmly.

She didn't want him with her. This was far too intimate an experience to share with a man who still might be living in the criminal world. A man who had looked her in the face and lied to her. She didn't want him near her baby.

"I can call a cab."

"I'm sure you can," he told her, keeping his voice even as he continued holding on to her, "but I'm still driving you. If you're worried about this Josiah guy, I'm sure he won't mind my getting you to the hospital. I'll call him for you once we get there if you like," he promised.

"I—" The rest of the words she'd intended to say faded as she sucked in her breath again, all but gagging with the effort. Practically panting, Eve shook her head in silent, adamant protest.

"I never realized you had this stubborn streak," he commented. "But you're going to the hospital and I'm taking you. End of story," he declared firmly. *Or maybe, just the beginning.*

"No, I'm not." She wasn't going anywhere, and not because she didn't want to. There was horror in her eyes as she said between her teeth, "The…baby's… coming."

They'd already established that. "I know that, that's why I'm—"

Adam stopped talking. He assessed her expression and the way Eve was squeezing his wrist, as if she was about to break it off at any second. He realized she was trying to unconsciously transfer the pain. Which meant her pain level had increased.

"You're having the baby right now, aren't you?" he concluded. Concern gripped him in its giant, callused hand.

It took Eve a couple of seconds to regain her voice. "You think?"

The moment she confirmed his suspicions, Adam picked Eve up into his arms. Beside them, Tessa began to leap about excitedly, jumping up and trying to become part of the game.

"Not now, dog," Adam ordered gruffly. Tessa stopped leaping. Instantly subdued, she glanced from him to her mistress. "Which way to your bedroom?"

Why was he asking her that? She couldn't focus her eyes or her brain. "It's upstairs. But I don't think…"

"It would help if you didn't talk, too," Adam told her,

annoyed that he wouldn't be able to get her to the hospital in time. "I've got to get you onto a bed."

She couldn't seem to get in enough air. As he began to climb the stairs, she laced her arms around his neck, afraid that he might drop her. "That's the way this whole thing started."

"Still got a sense of humor," he observed, a thread of optimism weaving through him. Even pregnant, she hardly felt as if she weighed anything, he thought. "That's a good sign."

She didn't want a sign, she wanted this to be over with.

The room temperature felt like it had gone up by at least ten degrees, if not more, and she felt as if she was caught between a pending implosion and an explosion. The pain now raced through her entire body, generating from her epicenter and radiating out like the unnerving aftershocks following an earthquake.

Was this what birthing was all about? Suddenly, she felt infinite empathy for the pets she treated. How could animals willingly mate after the first time, knowing that this kind of pain was what was in store for them?

"I'm…too…heavy," she protested.

"Actually, you're not," he told her just as he made it to the landing. There were several doors on either side. "Which way?"

Her breath was temporarily gone. Instead of telling him, she pointed to the first door on the left.

The door was already open. Moving as swiftly as he could, with the dog shadowing his every step, Adam crossed the threshold and placed Eve down on her bed.

The moment she felt the mattress beneath her, Eve

grabbed the comforter on either side of her, bunching it up beneath her frantically clutching fingers.

Adam saw her bite down on her lower lip.

"You *can* scream, you know," he told her, watching her struggle. "That doesn't make you any less of a mother—or a woman."

"I'm not screaming," she retorted with passion.

She absolutely refused to have her baby coming into the world with her screams ringing in his or her ears. But bottling up the pain wasn't easy.

It took her a second to realize that Adam was asking her something. Even her eyes felt as if they were sweating.

"What?" she demanded breathlessly.

"What's your doctor's name?" Adam repeated.

"Mudd," she gasped.

He almost laughed out loud. He sympathized with her feelings. He'd once had a doctor's assistant in one of the little border towns in Mexico digging a bullet out of his shoulder. He'd felt the same way about the man.

"No need for name calling," he told her, banking down his amusement. "What—?"

"Her name is Mudd," she repeated. Gritting her teeth, she gave him specifics. "Geraldine…Mudd."

He nodded, owning up to his mistake. "Okay. Sorry about that."

Adam took out his phone and pressed the key for Information. Instead of ringing, he heard the irritating sound that told him his call couldn't go through. One glance at the screen told him his signal was all but nonexistent. He swallowed a curse. The next second, Eve was grabbing the edge of his shirt. Before she could speak, another huge contraction had her arching her entire body up off the bed like a human tunnel.

She all but collapsed when the pain receded. "No time."

She knew her own body better than he did, Adam reasoned, flipping his phone closed again. He shoved it back into his pocket.

"Whatever you say. Don't worry." He did his best to sound reassuring despite the fact that he was worried himself. "I've had training."

"In what?" Her eyes were wide again as she looked at him.

His answer was carefully guarded, but he did want to assuage her fears. "In first aid and what to do if a woman goes into labor."

Was he telling the truth? But how could he be? "Drug dealing has gotten more complicated."

"I went to the Y. I like being prepared for all contingencies." It was a lie. He couldn't very well tell her that he'd taken the mandatory classes as part of his DEA training.

The next moment, any other questions she might have asked flew out of her head, chased out by the massive waves of pain sweeping over her. Sweat poured out of her even though the room was relatively cool.

She could feel her child pushing, trying to fight his or her way out.

With all her heart, she wished she could be bringing her baby into a better world than what waited for it. Wished that at least the baby would have not just a mother, but a father there, as well.

But the time for philosophical debates had long since passed.

In a vague, hot haze, she could feel Adam's hands on her, stripping off her underwear and pushing up the loose dress she was wearing.

Words, there were words. He was saying something to her. An apology? What was he apologizing for?

Oh, for having to undress her.

She laughed shortly. The time for that, too, was long gone. If she hadn't let him undress her in the first place, there would have been no need for him to undress her now.

"You're crowning," he declared, trying to mask his surprise.

He could feel excitement coursing through his veins. Despite the way she was behaving, he hadn't thought it possible for this process to be happening this quickly. If she'd been a race car, Eve would have literally gone from zero to sixty in a quarter of a heartbeat.

Oh, God, he hoped he could remember everything he'd been taught. Those lessons all seemed like he'd sat through them an eternity ago. He'd never had an occasion to put any of it into practice before.

Until now.

Taking a breath, he braced himself. "Okay, Eve, push."

Eve squeezed her eyes shut. She clutched the comforter, feeling the lace rip beneath her fingers as she held on to the material tightly and pushed for all she was worth. Through it all, she was vaguely aware of Tessa running back and forth near the foot of the bed.

Poor Tessa, the tension in the room had gotten to her, Eve thought.

"Okay, stop!" Adam ordered. "Stop!"

Eve fell back against the bed, her hair plastered to

the back of her neck, her head spinning almost wildly. "Is it here yet?"

Couldn't she tell the difference? he wondered, amazed. "No." It was all coming back to him, thank God. "I need you to relax and take a few deep breaths, then push again."

She did as he told her, knowing he was right even though she resented his presence, resented that he knew what to do. Resented him for bringing her to this state. Her body felt a kinship to a Thanksgiving wishbone being pulled in two separate directions. In agony, she was angry at the world.

"Now push, Eve," he was shouting at her. "C'mon, push!"

Exhaustion wore away her second wave of energy. She felt as if she had nothing left. Even so, she managed to muster together more from somewhere. Grunting as she followed orders, she pushed for all she was worth.

Again with nothing to show for it except possibly the vein she was certain had burst in her head.

Panting like a twenty-six-mile marathon runner at the end of the race, she fell against the bed again.

All too soon, she heard Adam asking, "Ready?"

If she had any strength, she would have hit him. "No," she cried hoarsely.

He was positioned to catch the baby when it emerged. Raising his eyes, he looked up at Eve. "I know this is hard—"

"How?" she demanded in an angry whisper. "How do you know?" He wasn't a woman, he had no right to say that he knew. He *didn't* know.

"Okay, I'm making an educated guess here," Adam

conceded. "But you can do this. I know you can do this. Women have been doing this since the beginning of time."

More proof that God wasn't a woman, Eve thought. But there really was no other choice. She had to do this or die. Propping herself up on her elbows, screwing her eyes shut, Eve bore down and pushed until she thought her head would pop off. And then she pushed some more.

Dying was beginning to sound like a very tempting option.

Chapter 5

"You're doing it, Eve!" Adam exclaimed excitedly, cheering her on. "You're doing it!"

It felt as if her insides were being ripped apart by some powerful, unseen hand. She squeezed her eyes shut so tightly, she saw concentric orbs of bright red and gold.

"I…know…" Eve panted. She could barely scrape together enough energy to push the words out of her mouth.

And then she heard it. A small, lusty wail.

Her baby? Was that coming from her baby? Or was she just hallucinating?

Belatedly, she realized that she still had her eyes shut. Her lashes were wet with perspiration and all but glued together.

When she opened her eyes, she saw what was in her estimation the most beautiful sight that had ever been created. Her baby in Adam's arms.

"What is it?" she asked breathlessly.

Unable to maintain her position a second longer, Eve's elbows went out from under her and she collapsed back onto the bed.

"Beautiful," Adam answered reverently, looking down into the dewy face of his daughter. He was completely mesmerized and enchanted. And utterly head over heels in love.

Had anyone asked, he would have said that his heart was impenetrable, that the only one who had ever managed to crack the exterior had been Eve. But this little being, this nothing-short-of-a-miracle that he had helped bring into the world, had seized his heart in her tiny hands the moment she made her debut.

He was in love with her, in love with this miracle who had come from nothing, who was the result of a chance, passionate coupling and a product malfunction.

"But what is it?" Eve asked, frustrated.

"It's a girl," he told her, still staring at the infant. He forced himself to tear his eyes away and look at Eve. "You have a daughter." He'd almost said "we" instead, but the very idea that the baby was half his still hadn't taken root. Besides, Eve had been the one to do all the work. The credit was hers.

He moved closer to Eve and tucked the naked newborn into her arms. Pressing the infant against her chest, awe instantly slid over Eve. She felt the newborn's warmth penetrating her skin.

"She's so little," Eve murmured in surprise, then looked up at Adam. "Where's the rest of her?"

The baby did seem little, Adam thought. Little and perfect. "She's whole, Eve."

"But it felt like I was giving birth to an elephant. The world's largest elephant," she amended. This was a little bit of a thing she should have been able to push out on a sneeze.

Adam laughed softly. "This is all of her," he assured Eve. Taking a step back, he glanced toward the hall, as if to check if the rest of the world was still there after this miracle had taken place. "I need to get a knife to cut the umbilical cord." He looked at Eve uncertainly. "Will you be okay if I leave you for a couple of minutes?" he asked.

The bonding was instantaneous, as was the surge of motherly pride and love. Eve couldn't get herself to tear her eyes away from this brand-new human being in her arms even for a second.

"We'll be fine, won't we, Brooklyn?" she asked the infant.

About to leave, the name stopped Adam cold in his tracks. He looked at her over his shoulder. "Brooklyn?" he echoed.

Eve nodded. Very gingerly, she skimmed her fingertips along the baby's clenched fist. Five fingers, there were five fingers, she assured herself. On both hands. She'd never felt anything so soft, she thought. Like snowflakes. Precious, precious snowflakes.

"My father was born there," she explained. "I always liked the sound of the name."

"Brooklyn," he repeated, rolling it over on his

tongue. Looking back at her and the baby, he slowly nodded. "Not bad." But right now, the baby and Eve were still very much attached. He needed to sterilize a knife and separate them. "I'll be right back," he promised.

Still looking at her daughter's face, Eve smiled. "We're not going anywhere."

He had to admit he liked the sound of that.

The moment he left, Eve raised her eyes to the doorway to be sure that he was gone.

"That was your father," she whispered to the infant in her arms. "He's a little unusual and he needs some work, but maybe with you here, we can fix him and make him into a good dad." She took a deep, fortifying breath. Her lungs had finally stopped aching. "At least it's worth a try."

She knew it was the euphoria talking, but it gave her something to hang on to.

Adam was back faster than she thought possible. As he'd said, he had a knife in his hand. But the look on his face as he regarded her was slightly dubious, as if he wasn't happy with what he was about to do.

"What's wrong?" Eve asked.

He regarded the knife and then her. He had no problem digging out a bullet in his own arm, but the thought of using a knife on her for any reason suddenly didn't seem like such a good idea.

"I don't know if this is going to hurt. Either of you," he added.

Considering what she'd just gone through, she felt she was pretty much beyond hurt. "Just do it and get it over with."

But he made no move to comply. "Maybe I should wait for the paramedics."

"What paramedics?" The euphoric bubble around her burst. Her eyes widened. When had he had time to place the call? "You called the paramedics?"

"Yes." He'd made the call in the kitchen. "I can't just toss the two of you into the back of my car or have you ride to the hospital on the handlebars of my motorcycle." The last was just an exaggeration. He *had* no motorcycle, at least, not here.

As far as she was concerned, the discussion was all just moot. "Why do we have to ride *anything* to the hospital?" she argued. "It's over, the baby's here." As she referred to her daughter, she couldn't suppress the smile that came to her lips.

"You both need to be checked out," he told her in a no-nonsense voice that said this wasn't up for debate.

Exhausted though she was, Eve felt her back go up. Where did he get off, telling her what she was supposed to do? "Nobody put you in charge."

"I got the position by default because you're not being sensible," he informed her. Seeing her frown, he added diplomatically, "It's understandable. You've just been through an ordeal and condensed eighteen hours of labor into about ten minutes flat. Anyone would have been addled by that—"

She cut him off. "I'm not addled, I'm fine. We're both fine," she insisted, looking at her daughter who now dozed. "And we don't need to go to the hospital." She just wanted to be left alone to enjoy her daughter. And rest.

His eyes narrowed. Something was off. For an ordinarily sensible woman, she was protesting too much. "What are you afraid of?"

"I'm not afraid," Eve retorted, but he kept on watching her as if he didn't believe her, as if he was waiting for her to tell him the truth. She pressed her lips together and looked up toward the ceiling. It kept the tears from flowing. "The last time I was in a hospital, it was to see the E.R. doctor pronounce my father dead. I just don't think I can handle being there."

The sound of approaching sirens pushed their way into the stillness, swelling in volume.

"Too late," Adam told her. "Besides, this is a completely different situation. Don't you want to know if Brooklyn's all right?" he asked her. With his free hand, he stroked the baby's head ever so gently. Something warm moved through him. He felt fiercely protective of this little being, instinctively knowing that he would kill for her if it came down to that. "I mean, she looks perfect, but just to be sure, you need to have a pediatrician confirm that."

She didn't think it was possible, not after all Adam had put her through, not after all the disappointment she'd felt when she discovered that he'd been lying to her the whole time they'd spent together, but her heart softened to hear him call their daughter perfect.

And she knew he was right. Her baby needed to be checked out by a doctor.

Much as she didn't want to, she had to go to the hospital, not for herself, but for her baby's sake. For Brooklyn.

She nodded toward the knife he'd brought. "I want you to cut the cord before they get here."

"Okay."

With one quick, clean movement, he severed the physical connection between mother and child. The moment Adam placed the knife down, he heard the front doorbell ringing.

"Looks like the cavalry has arrived," he told her. Turning on his heel, he left the room to admit the paramedics.

"No," she said softly to her daughter, glancing toward Adam's retreating back, "the cavalry's already here."

Rather than riding with Eve and the baby in the ambulance, or opting to go back home now that he'd helped Eve give birth to their baby, Adam decided to follow the ambulance to the hospital in his car.

Arriving at the hospital a half beat behind the paramedics, he left his vehicle parked in the lot designated for emergency room patients and stood at the back of the ambulance before the doors even opened. When they did, the first thing he saw was Eve's face. She was looking for him. When their eyes met, her smile widened.

It still got to him, that thousand-watt smile that always seemed to light up the room, or, in this case, the inside of the ambulance.

And the inside of him.

He supposed there was only so much a heart could be hardened.

This wasn't good, he admonished in the next moment. He needed a clear head to do what he was doing. Any distraction could prove fatal, not just to his operation, but to him, as well. He shouldn't be here.

Eve didn't need him. She was in professional hands now. These people were trained for this. They could more than take care of her and anything that she needed. As long as Eve was here, in the middle of a bustling hospital, she'd be out of harm's way.

Besides, as far as he actually knew, no one in this region knew about their connection. His connection, the self-centered college student, Sederholm, didn't know about Eve. This was all a preemptive strike on his part.

But he lived the life too long to be at ease, to hope that everything went well and that there would be no mishaps, no reason to believe that either Eve or the baby would be in jeopardy. He'd learned that when one of the agents had grown lax during the last undercover operation, he had gotten blown away. Literally. From where he stood, it was far better to be safe than live with a lifetime of regret.

"I need you to call Vera for me," she said to him the moment the paramedics mobilized the gurney, snapping the wheels in place. They immediately began to guide the gurney in through the automatic sliding doors.

Adam hurried to keep pace with the gurney. The name she'd just tossed in his direction meant nothing to him. "Vera?"

"Dr. Vera Lee. She's the veterinarian who works with me at the Laguna Animal Hospital. She's going to have to take over the appointments and have Susannah reschedule the ones that aren't emergencies until I can get back to work."

Which wouldn't be for a while if he had anything to say about it, he thought. Childbirth might be natural, but it could knock the hell out of a woman and Eve needed to give herself some time to recover.

"Susannah?" he repeated. Another name that meant nothing to him.

"Susannah Reyes. She's my tech and she doubles as a receptionist." Wanda Peeples had been her father's technician and receptionist for thirty years, but when he died, the woman, already in her seventies, had retired. Grief-stricken, she'd debated selling the practice for all of five hours, then decided to take over, rebuilding it from the ground up.

Frustrated, Eve shook her head. "I really thought I was going to have more time."

Who was it that said life was what happens while you were busy making plans? "Life's full of surprises," Adam told her.

And he should know that better than anyone, he thought, looking down at the infant cradled in her arms.

"All right, I'll call Vera and Susannah. Anything else?"

"Yes." She took a breath, then raised her head. Her eyes met his. "Thank you."

Adam hadn't been expecting that. Hearing Eve voice her gratitude brought a smile to his lips. "You're welcome."

The moment was quickly dissipated by the authoritative, stocky nurse who came up to him and hooked her arm through his. "You the husband?" the woman demanded.

Eve spoke up before he had a chance to. "He's the father."

Picking up on the difference, the nurse declared, "Good enough," and thrust a clipboard with several sheets clipped to it at him. "I need you to fill out some information."

Adam quickly scanned the top sheet. There was no way that he knew even half the information that was being asked. "Look, I can't—"

"I'm preregistered," Eve called out as the paramedics, rattling off pertinent information regarding both mother and child, turned her over to an orderly and another nurse. The duo paused for a moment as the gurney changed hands.

"Saved you some trouble," the stocky nurse mumbled to Adam, taking back the clipboard. Then, as Adam turned to continue following Eve's gurney, the woman placed her hand against his chest, stopping him in his tracks. "You can't go with her just yet," she informed him. And then she softened just a little. "They need to settle her in first, then they'll call for you."

Adam was accustomed to making his own rules as he went along, to coming and going as he saw fit without waiting for someone else's okay.

But this wasn't the kind of situation he ordinarily found himself in. Not wanting to draw attention to himself, he had no recourse but to go along with procedure. "What floor is maternity on?"

"Fifth." She clamped her mouth shut, as if she'd just given away a state secret. "But you can wait here," she went on, her eyes daring him to contradict the edict.

"I'll wait on the fifth floor," he told the woman. There was no arguing with his tone.

"All right, suit yourself. Just give the nurse at the desk your name when you get there."

He inclined his head, as if she had been the one to win and not him. "Yes, ma'am."

As he walked to the bank of elevators located to the

side, he heard the nurse mutter under her breath, "If I was just twenty years younger…"

A small, amused smile curved his mouth.

"How do you feel?" he asked Eve, walking into her private room.

It was more than thirty minutes later and he had begun to think that something had gone wrong. But then an intern had found him and gave him the all clear sign, telling him the number of Eve's room. He lost no time in getting there.

She'd just begun to doze off. The sound of Adam's voice temporarily banished any thought of sleep. She'd started to think that he'd taken the opportunity to leave the hospital.

That he hadn't coaxed a smile from her.

"Like I've been run over by a truck. Twice." Eve took a deep breath and pushed herself up into a sitting position. "They said that Brooklyn's fine."

Adam nodded. He'd been to the nursery before coming to her room. "I know. I asked."

She should have known he would. The man didn't believe in leaving stones unturned. "You're thorough."

Crossing to her, he stood at her bedside and struggled against the temptation to brush the hair away from her cheek. Instead, Adam shoved his hands into his pockets.

"Keeps the mistakes at a minimum," he told her.

She raised her eyes to his. For a moment, she was silent. And then she said, "At least some of them."

Was she telling him that she thought of their having made love as a mistake? That would mean that she considered the baby a mistake, which wasn't the impression he'd gotten. He'd seen love in her eyes when she looked down at Brooklyn.

"Some of them," he echoed.

She ran her fingers along the top of her hospital gown. There was so much she wanted to say, so much she wanted to ask him and somehow resolve. But she was so very tired again. Far too tired to think clearly.

As she fought off the drugging demands of fatigue, Eve tried to remember what it was that she'd asked him to do. And then it came to her.

"Did you call Vera? I didn't give you her number," she realized out loud.

"I found it," he assured her. "And I called her. She wanted to know who I was."

She looked at him warily. "And what did you tell her?"

"The truth," he said simply. "That I was someone you used to know."

"That's not the truth." Although she fervently wished that it was. "I didn't know you." *And still don't,* she added silently. "I thought I did, but I didn't."

"We can talk about that some other time if you want to," he told her, cutting her off. He glanced at his watch. It was almost two in the morning—as Vera had pointed out none too happily when he'd called her—until he'd explained why he was calling. "Right now, you need your rest."

It just wasn't in her to argue with him. She knew he'd win. "I am tired," she agreed.

"I'll see you tomorrow, Eve."

It was a perfunctory remark. Right now, he really didn't know if he was coming back, at least not in such a way where she could see him. And he did have work to attend to, both his actual job and what he did in order to maintain a cover for the outside world. There were times when his double life really got to be confusing. The less she knew, the better for everyone. He couldn't jeopardize the mission, not even for her.

Besides, he was fairly sure the woman didn't completely trust him. She would be better off if he stayed away as much as he could.

Bending over, he pressed a kiss to Eve's forehead. "Get some sleep," he instructed just before he started to walk away.

He was almost at the door when he heard her call his name.

"Adam?"

Turning around, he waited for her to continue. Did she have a lingering craving and want him to bring her back a pound of pistachios or some licorice? "Yes?"

"Stay with me. Just for a few minutes," she added, anticipating being turned down. "I don't want to be alone just yet."

Was she having doubts about what she'd just let herself in for, becoming a mother? He heard that a lot of new mothers suddenly worried about that once the euphoria wore away.

He retraced his steps to her bedside. "Sure."

Pulling up a chair next to the bed, he swung it around and straddled it, then waited for Eve to drift off to sleep.

Chapter 6

An ache woke her up. It shot through her entire body, from the very roots of her hair down to the tips of her toes. All except for two of her fingernails—one on each hand—and those felt numb because she'd clutched so fiercely at her comforter while pushing out her daughter.

Her daughter. She had a daughter?

She had a daughter.

Her eyes flew open, the very act instantly divorcing her from the dream she'd been having.

She didn't need to remember, she knew the dream by heart. It was the same dream that had invaded a third of her nights in the last eight months. A dream that echoed what she'd felt that one glorious night that she and Adam had made love.

Eve blew out a breath. She hadn't had that dream for at least a couple of weeks now and had begun to nurse the hope that she was finally over it.

Finally over him.

Having Adam pop back into her life had brought the dream back in vivid living color—both the bad and the good.

Adam.

Last night's events came rushing back to her, assaulting her brain and sending her system into high alert. She couldn't let her guard down. Now that she knew what he was, she had to remain vigilant—at least, until she was sure that he'd changed.

If only…

As she remembered the last words that had passed between them, her eyes darted toward the chair where he'd sat down.

It was empty.

A sinking feeling set in and she railed against it. How lame could she have been, asking him to stay with her a little while longer? What in heaven's name had gotten into her? Nothing had changed—and probably he hadn't, either. She wanted Adam to go, not stay. So why had she suddenly felt so vulnerable? Why had she asked him to stay with her like a child who was afraid of the dark?

A noise came from the doorway and she glanced over, half hoping—

Idiot!

A blonde nurse walked in. She looked as if she was about twenty-two. A young two-twenty at that. The nurse pushed a see-through bassinette before her.

"Someone here wants to see her mommy," the nurse all but chirped cheerfully.

Eve squinted ever so slightly, reading the nurse's name tag: Kathy.

As Kathy parked the bassinette at the foot of the bed, she scanned the room. "Your husband stepped out?" she asked.

It took Eve a second to make the connection. "He's not my husband," she corrected.

"Oh." The response seemed to squelch the nurse's enthusiasm, but just for the barest moment. And then the insuppressible cheerfulness returned. "Well, anyway, he seemed very devoted to you." Picking the baby up, Kathy made a few soothing noises to the infant and then placed the tiny bundle into Eve's arms.

Eve hated the fact that she was distracted even the slightest bit, but the nurse's comment had aroused her curiosity. She patted the baby's bottom as she asked, "What makes you say that?"

Kathy moved around the room, drawing back the curtains at the window, tucking the blanket in on one side. She seemed as if she needed to be in perpetual motion.

"Well, for one thing, he stayed here most of the night. He was sitting by your bed when I came on my shift this morning," she added.

Eve saw only one reason for that. "He must've fallen asleep."

But Kathy shook her head, a wistful smile curving the corners of her mouth. "Looked pretty wide-awake to me. Gail said he'd been there all night, just watching you sleep."

"Gail?"

"The nurse who was on before me." She smiled down into Brooklyn's face. Wide-awake, the infant appeared to absorb her surroundings. "The baby looks like him," Kathy commented. And then she raised her eyes quickly to look at her patient, as if she realized that she'd just tripped over her tongue. "He is the father, right?"

"Yes," Eve said quietly, gazing at her daughter's face. A face that had more in common with Adam than with her. "He's the father."

A shade under six feet with an almost painfully thin body, Danny Sederholm leaned indolently against the side of the cement steps of the renovated campus library. The renovation had been conducted, in part, thanks to his father and his uncle's generous contributions. Both were former alumni of the prestigious college, as was his mother. It made coasting easier.

The student's small, deep-set brown eyes unabashedly looked him over and took renewed assessment as he approached. Adam struggled to keep his contempt and loathing to himself.

"You look like hell. Something wrong?" Sederholm asked, trying to sound high-handed.

The marbles-for-brains twenty-two-year-old was leagues away from the kind of kid he'd been at that age, Adam thought. Circumstances had forced him to be a man early. Sederholm, he judged, would never be one no matter how old he was.

"Don't worry, it's nothing I can't handle," he told the snide senior, his tone firmly closing the door on any further speculation regarding the situation.

"Do I look worried?" Sederholm challenged. "Hey, as long as it don't interfere with 'business,'" he emphasized the word haughtily, "I don't care if you're juggling flying monkeys."

"'As long as it "don't" interfere?'" Adam knew he should let the comment slide, but bad grammar always got under his skin, especially when uttered by someone who gave himself airs. "How much did you say your father was paying for your education? Because whatever it is, it's way too much."

Sederholm's face darkened. "Like I don't have better things to do than go sit in a lousy auditorium with a bunch of competitive geeks." He puffed up his chest. "I'm making more money now than my old man ever did at my age—or when he graduated."

Adam knew exactly what tuition was at the school. It was part of his background research. "Then why would you bother registering? The $40K this costs could be better spent."

Sederholm shrugged, his large, bony shoulders moving carelessly beneath a sweater that would have set him back two months' pay. "It's his money and that's what he wants to do with it."

Adam saw through the blasé remark. "Can't figure a way to siphon it off, can you?" he guessed, not bothering to hide his amusement.

"I don't want to," the student snapped at him, annoyed. "In case your tiny brain can't figure it out, an Ivy League college campus is the perfect place to run my enterprise. As an undergraduate student," he spread his hands out wide, "I fit right in."

Adam saw a few obstacles to the senior's "brilliant"

plan. "You have to pass a few tests to stay in the game, don't you?"

Sederholm snorted, more than a little pleased with himself. "I've got that covered. There's this guy who, for the right price, can write an A-plus paper on any subject you throw at him."

There were always plenty of those around, Adam thought. Even when he was going to school. "What about tests?"

The student's smile was condescendingly smug. "I've got that covered, too." He lifted his chin, a lofty look in his eyes. "Why all the questions?"

"Just curious." Because that didn't seem to satisfy his contact, Adam added, "When I grow up, I want to be just like you," allowing only a drop of sarcasm to leak through.

Initially, the senior seemed to take the words as a compliment, but the frown that soon unfurled told Adam that the arrogant drug dealer realized he was being ridiculed.

"I can have you wiped off the face of the earth with a snap of my fingers," Sederholm threatened him haughtily, snapping his fingers to illustrate.

Obviously, the little twerp had probably come close to OD'ing on classic gangster movies, most likely starting with Cagney and Bogart. For two cents, he would have loved to squash the snotty senior like a bug, but he knew bigger things were at stake here than just mollifying his temper—no matter how good it might feel at the time. Like it or not—and he didn't— he needed this jerk to get hooked up to the head importer whose identity was still unknown to him.

"Before you snap again," Adam told him, lightly

catching hold of Sederholm's wrist, "I'd like to place an order for my people."

"Business before pleasure," the cocky student declared with an obliging nod of his head. Adam released his hand, wishing he could be wringing Sederholm's neck instead. "You know," Sederholm said, the smile on his lips as genuine as the smile on a cobra, "one of these days, you're going to push my buttons too hard."

I'm counting on it, kid, Adam thought just before he gave the college senior a list of just how much he was looking to score.

Sederholm seemed properly impressed. "That's almost twice as much as you bought last time."

Adam made certain to appear unfazed. "Word gets around. You've got a good product."

Sederholm nodded, preening. "Yeah, it's damn good all right." And then he frowned slightly. "But if you want that much of it, you might have to wait a little," he warned.

"If this is too much for you to handle, I can always take my business—"

"I didn't say it was too much for me," Sederholm cut in angrily. "It's just going to take a little longer to get it all together, that's all." Pausing, he was apparently trying to think, but there were times, like now, when the process appeared difficult for him. Undoubtedly, he'd been sampling "the product" again. "When do you need the stuff by?"

Adam eyed the student. "I was thinking now."

Sederholm was taken aback. And then he laughed. It was a nasty sound. "Right, like I carry that kind of stash on me. What are you, crazy?"

Again, Adam shrugged nonchalantly. "Got a lot of antsy customers."

Sederholm shut his eyes and scrubbed his hand over his face. "How's tomorrow sound?"

"Not as good as today," Adam replied without hesitation, "but it'll do. Where and when?"

"I'll call you," he said cavalierly.

Adam resisted the urge to pat Sederholm on the head, the way he might have to a dim-witted toady who'd tried too hard. He didn't want to put the kid off until the sting went down, and right now, the timetable was still unclear.

So instead, he smiled complacently and said, "You do that."

Adam waited until he was back in his car, driving north on University Road and away from the forty-five-year-old college campus before he put in a call to his handler via his Bluetooth.

"Looks like the plan's working," he told the man. "Sederholm's going to his source sometime between today and tomorrow."

"The big fish?" he heard Hugh ask.

He only wished. "Right now, it sounds like the medium fish. But it's only a matter of time. We keep doing business with him and we place an order big enough, medium fish is going to have to get in contact with big fish," Adam theorized.

"And then we'll reel them in." He heard Hugh allow himself a sliver of optimism. "Meanwhile, you know what to do."

"Yeah." He knew what to do. Continue leading his double life—and deceiving Eve. The longer he stayed undercover like this, the greater the odds were that someone was going to get hurt. One way or another, it seemed inevitable.

"Something wrong?" He and Hugh had been together long enough for him to know that though it didn't sound it, Hugh was concerned.

"I'm going to need a little time away from the job today," Adam told his handler.

"All right," Hugh allowed cautiously. There was leeway within their framework. "How little and is it going to get in the way of anything?"

"An hour, maybe less. Around one," Adam added. "And no, it's not going to get in the way of anything." *Just my conscience,* he said silently. "I've got someone covering for me at the bookstore." He didn't bother adding that the woman, somewhere in her sixties, was a dynamo who had reorganized all his shelves the first week she was hired. "You're going to have to get someone to keep tabs on Sederholm. The kid drives a 2009 silver Lexus SC 430 convertible. It shouldn't be too much of a problem spotting him wherever he goes."

Adam heard Hugh whistle. "Wish my mommy and daddy gave me a sixty-five-thousand-dollar car."

"More like sixty-seven point six," Adam corrected. Handing over the keys to that kind of vehicle to an immature brat seemed unfathomable to him.

"I can get Chesterfield to follow him," Hugh told him. "Chesterfield likes surveillance work."

Surveillance work was something he really hated. Though he considered himself tenacious, sitting in a car for hours on end drove him up a wall. He could literally feel life slipping through his fingers on a stakeout. He was a man who valued action, not stagnation.

"Different strokes for different folks, I guess," Adam commented. "More power to him."

"That's what makes the world go around," Hugh agreed. The next moment, the line went dead. Adam closed his cell phone. He was accustomed to Hugh's calls. The handler wasn't one to stand on ceremony. When he was done, he was done.

One o'clock had Adam hurrying down the corridor of the maternity ward. He carried a bouquet of red roses in one hand and a teddy bear sporting a pink bow and a pink tutu in the other. Neither, he knew, was exactly very original, but the offerings were the best he could do on short notice. Undertaking yet another life, bringing him to a grand total of three, was running him ragged.

Eve didn't even know his real last name. He was still lying to her and calling it the truth. How was she going to handle that? he thought uneasily. How was she going to feel when she found out that all of this, the second-hand bookstore, the so-called life of a drug dealer, all of that was just a setup, a sham, a means to an end?

Why was he even wondering about that, he upbraided himself. He would be out of her life before that happened, not settling in for good.

If a part of him yearned for love and family, well, he would have to bank it down. He knew what he was signing on for when he volunteered for this kind of work. There wasn't going to be a happy ending for him after two hours, when the credits rolled. This was real life and it was gritty.

When he reached Eve's room, he heard voices coming from inside. Specifically, a male voice. Was that her doctor?

The moment he opened the door, Adam knew the small, trim, older man, dressed in tan slacks and a dark blue sports jacket, was not a doctor. Doctors were given to scrubs and lab coats, not expensive suits he was fairly certain came from a high-end shop. Despite the unseasonably warm weather, the man wore a tie. The tidy Van Dyke gray beard he sported made him look old enough to be her grandfather. But Adam knew she didn't have one.

Who was this man?

Adam cleared his throat, crossed the threshold and gave the door a little push with his elbow, closing it behind him. When Eve looked his way, he said, "Hi."

Everything inside of her lit up before she could tell it not to. Why didn't she know better?

"Hi," she answered. Her eyes strayed toward the bouquet. There were at least a dozen and a half roses swaddled in green and white tissue paper with sprigs of baby's breath tucked in between the blossoms. "Are those for me?" Eve prodded when Adam made no effort to give her the bouquet.

"Well, they're not for me," the man on the other side of her bed observed. "For one thing, this young man had no way of knowing that I would be here."

"They're for you," Adam murmured, feeling damn awkward as he almost thrust the bouquet at her. This was a bad idea, he thought. He should have realized that she'd have company. She was far too outgoing a woman not to.

"They're lovely," she said, inhaling deeply. They were the fragrant kind, her favorite type of roses.

Adam could feel steely gray eyes regarding him for a long moment, obviously assessing him.

"And you are?" Eve's dapper companion finally asked as he passed the man while crossing to the sink. Opening the cabinet below, Adam took out a pink pitcher and filled it with water, then brought it over to Eve. Only once he deposited the bouquet, stripped of its tissue paper, into the pitcher and placed it on her table did he answer the man's question. "Adam. Adam Smythe."

The look on the older man's gaunt face seemed to say that he knew better. "Of course you are," he said with the air of man humoring someone of far less mental acuity. "Well, Adam Smith—"

"Smythe," Adam corrected, giving it the standard British pronunciation.

"Sorry, *Smythe*," the older man amended, "I'm Josiah Turner."

Adam's eyes widened and he looked at Eve. "That's Josiah Turner?"

Until that moment, she'd forgotten that she'd referred to Josiah as the man she was currently involved with. Eve pressed her lips together. "I was in labor. I didn't know what I was saying."

Josiah's voice warmed as he turned toward Eve. "I've known Eve since she was a little girl. I'd bring my dogs in to be treated by her father and Eve would be there, soaking up everything her father did like a sponge. I knew she'd be a good veterinarian even then." The steely eyes narrowed as Josiah shifted his focus back to him. "And how do you know her?"

Adam had no idea how much or how little Eve wanted

him to admit, so he kept the narrative vague. "I met her when she came into my bookstore in Santa Barbara. She was looking to buy a first edition Mark Twain for her father. I had an original copy of *A Connecticut Yankee in King Arthur's Court.* Just yesterday I ran into her again." Adam looked at Eve. "Small world."

Josiah obviously had another take on the events. "You were stalking her?"

The accusation, politely worded, stunned Adam. "No," he denied vehemently. Who was this man?

Josiah didn't seem particularly convinced or contrite. Instead, his shoulders shifted in what constituted a minor shrug.

"My mistake." However, he gave no indication that he was ready to move on to another topic. "So you both just *happen* to transplant yourselves to the same city— or are you here on a visit, Adam?"

Adam felt as if he was being subtly grilled. "I relocated my shop."

"Interesting," Josiah commented. "And what is your shop called?"

"New Again," Adam told him.

Josiah nodded. "I must look you up when I get the chance. As it happens, I like first editions myself. Of course," he slanted a glance toward Eve, and Adam noted that the older man's look softened considerably as he did so, "I'm old enough to have been around for a great many of these books when they *were* first editions."

"You're not that old, Josiah," Eve insisted with a warm smile.

The man leaned forward and patted her hand. "You have no idea how old I really am, my dear. It's a state secret—and I intend to keep it that way." He took her hand in his. "Since you have a visitor, I'll take my leave now. But I'll be back tonight. Call me if there's anything special I can bring you when I return." He kissed her hand, then released it as he straightened. The smile on his face vanished as he regarded Adam. "Adam," he acknowledged with a nod of his head, and with that, moving with considerable grace and agility, Josiah Turner made his way to the door.

Adam watched the door close behind the man. "That's quite a character. Is he a relative?"

"In name only." When Adam looked at her quizzically, she explained, "When I was a little girl, I thought he was my father's uncle so I called him my great-uncle. He's a very sweet man. He had a daughter, but she's married and living out of the country. England, I think. I'm the only 'family' he has, if you don't count Lucas."

"Lucas?"

"His driver. Actually, Lucas is more of an assistant slash companion, although I doubt Josiah would call him that."

"How did he know you were in the hospital?" Adam asked, rearranging the roses so that they were more even. He had a thing about symmetry.

"I forgot he had an appointment this morning," she said ruefully. "Annual shots for his Doberman, Edgar. When he found Vera there instead of me, he asked her where I was and she told him that Brooklyn arrived early. He brought the baby a present." She'd assumed that the old man would, but she hadn't been prepared for what the gift turned out to be. She glanced down at the card Josiah had brought. "I've got to find a way to make him take it back."

Eve didn't strike him as the type to refuse a gift. Doing so would most likely offend the man and that didn't seem like something she would be willing to do. "Why? What is it?"

Instead of telling him, Eve took the card out of its envelope and opened it. She held up what had been tucked inside the card.

Taking it from her, he turned it around. It was a check. A rather large check. Adam looked at her incredulously. "He gave you a check for twenty thousand dollars?"

What kind of man just hands over a check for that amount of money?

She nodded, taking the check and putting it back into its envelope. For now, she put it into the drawer of her side table. It made her uneasy just looking at it. "It's the tuition to an exclusive nursery school," she told him. "He told me he had a friend who could get her placed near the top of the waiting list."

Adam looked at her sharply.

Chapter 7

Because of the deceptions he was forced to employ in his daily life, Adam's suspicions were immediately aroused. "Is this Josiah guy usually so generous?"

It was the largest monetary gift Josiah had ever given her, but as she thought back, Eve realized that the man had been generous to her over the years. There'd been a sizable "contribution" to her college fund when she'd gone off to become a veterinarian. And every birthday and Christmas were observed with cards. The cards were never empty.

"Pretty much," she confirmed. "From what my father indicated, Josiah has a sizable amount of money, more than he needs."

"How much is 'sizable'?" he asked her. Was Josiah involved in this drug cartel he was looking to bring down? Stranger things had turned out to be true. Maybe this man with no visible means of support actually made a living importing drugs.

"Enough," she answered carefully. She didn't like his tone. An uneasiness began to weave itself through her. She could feel herself growing very protective of Josiah. "What is it you're thinking?"

Adam shrugged. He couldn't very well come out and tell her what he was thinking. "Just wondering how he made his money, that's all."

That wasn't all. She was willing to bet on it. "The old-fashioned way," she answered tersely.

He'd annoyed her. That wasn't his intention. Adam backtracked and guessed teasingly, "He stole it? Printed it?"

"He earned it. Josiah was some kind of a business-man before he retired."

"What kind of business?" he asked casually.

"I don't know. But he did a lot of traveling, I know that. And when he did, he'd board the dogs with my dad." She drew in a breath, then let it out again slowly as she regarded the table over her bed and the check that was inside the drawer. "But I still can't accept a check that large."

"Sure you can." He saw the look that came into her eyes. She probably thought he wanted to use it. "Still don't trust me, do you?"

"You have to admit, it's a little hard." Especially when one minute Adam was all but accusing Josiah of being a robber baron, the next he's pushing her to take the money the man had given her. Just which way was Adam leaning? And why?

Adam inclined his head. "I can see how you might feel that way," he allowed.

And if you ever find out the rest of it, you really *won't trust me.*

Knowing how she might react if she found out the truth weighed him down. He found himself wishing that he could just be himself, in a position to tell her he was a law enforcement officer. But it was the undercover work that got drugs off the streets and provided the information that sent the dealers and suppliers to prison. He had to remember the game plan—and it didn't include falling for a civilian.

"Josiah didn't seem like the kind of man who would take kindly to having his gifts refused," Adam continued out loud. "If you don't want to use it for the baby, you can always donate the money he gave you to a charity—anonymously or even in Turner's name."

"To a charity," Eve repeated, rolling the idea over in her mind. She had to admit that Adam had come up with a decent, win-win suggestion. She knew that Josiah meant well, but she was hardly in a bad way. Her father's practice was a very established one and she could more than afford to take good care of her new daughter with the income she generated.

Adam's smile was encouraging. If only it wasn't so damn sensual, she thought. "Yes," he said. "To a charity."

She raised her eyes to his. "And not to you."

That caught him up short. But then, what did he expect? She thought he was a drug dealer. Reformed or not, that didn't exactly put him in the same league with martyrs and saints. And philanthropists.

"Why would you think that?" he asked.

"Because I'm not exactly all that clear about who or what you are."

The situation pained him more than he would have ever expected, but he could do nothing about it—at least, not yet. After this sting went down, then maybe he could tell her some things. Not everything, but enough to make her understand that he wasn't the devil assuming a pleasant form.

"Since that seems to be a stumbling block for you, why don't we just set that aside for the time being?" he suggested. "Let's just leave it at my wanting to come by to give you those." He nodded at the roses in the pitcher. "And to see how you were doing."

He sounded as if he was about to go. "You're leaving?"

It was better that way, he thought. For both of them. "I've got to get back to the store," he told her. "The sales clerk I hired might feel a little overwhelmed being in the store alone for so long."

"Oh? Doesn't he or she like books?" She was stalling, but who knew if she'd see him again once he walked out that door. Suddenly she wasn't ready to say goodbye.

"She," Adam specified. "And she doesn't like books, she loves them. That's just the trouble. Jennifer's busy reading instead of assisting customers." He laughed shortly. Now that the woman had organized everything, she'd dived right into worshipful reading. "She's practically ignoring them because they're cutting into her reading time."

He'd already asked Hugh to send him someone from the department to act as an assistant, in case he had to quickly "take care of business" during normal work hours. Hugh had told him he'd look into it.

Eve nodded. Without realizing it, she wrapped her arms around the teddy bear he'd brought, holding it close to her. The softness against her chin penetrated, and she flushed.

"I'll see that Brooklyn gets this," she promised, moving the teddy bear to one side.

"Good." Adam began to walk away, but he got no farther than ten steps when he abruptly turned around and doubled back. Reaching her bed, he framed her face and kissed her. The kiss was quick—he couldn't allow himself to linger, didn't trust himself to linger—but it still left an impression. On both of them. "Give her that, too."

"Not until she turns eighteen," Eve answered breathlessly, then realized her error as her words replayed themselves in her head. Her eyes darted to his. Damn it, why couldn't she just keep her mouth shut around him? She'd given too much away.

So what? she silently demanded the next minute. It wasn't as if Adam wouldn't have guessed that a very large piece of her heart still belonged to him, despite everything. Her problem was that she had a face that couldn't keep a secret.

Adam knew he should be on his way. For more than one reason. And yet, he found himself lingering a moment longer. "The baby's okay, right?"

"She's perfect."

"And you, the doctor says you're all right, too?"

Her own doctor had stopped by this morning, right after she'd woken up. Dr. Mudd had expressed surprise that she had delivered so early—and so quickly to boot. It wasn't unheard of, she'd told Eve, but it wasn't the norm, especially with first babies.

Eve smiled. "She said I'm none the worse for wear—just a little sore."

"So when are you being discharged?"

The doctor had given her a choice of tomorrow or the day after. She'd chosen sooner rather than later. "Tomorrow."

Adam nodded, more to himself than to her as he began rescheduling things in his head. "When?"

"Before noon."

That was doable. Especially if Hugh came through with someone. "Eleven-thirty work for you?"

"I don't— Why?" she asked, confused. And then it dawned on her. "Are you planning on taking us home?"

He couldn't gauge her tone, and her expression just registered surprise. "I thought, unless you made other arrangements, that I would, yes."

With everything so new and in fast-forward mode, she hadn't been able to think that far ahead yet. Now that she did, she supposed she could have Vera or Susannah take her home. And if something prevented that, she was fairly certain that Josiah would be more than delighted to come to her rescue.

None of these options made her skin tinge the way it did when she thought about Adam taking her home. That wasn't a good sign.

Eve pressed her lips together, doing what she could to seem indifferent, hoping she carried it off. "I don't want to inconvenience you."

"No inconvenience," Adam assured her, unconsciously flashing the smile that sent her stomach into a spin-dry cycle. "Okay, it's settled. I'll be here tomorrow before noon to take you and Brooklyn home," he promised, then forced himself to leave.

Even though he really didn't want to.

He was fifteen minutes late.

The meeting with his handler had run long and then the near-noon traffic seemed to conspire against him, moving slower than an aged inch worm.

On top of that, he'd had to park outside the hospital grounds because, apparently, everyone and his brother had decided that today was a good day to pay someone a visit. Twenty minutes of circling around the lots hadn't yielded a single empty space. He parked down the street, then ran back to the hospital.

Because waiting for an elevator would eat up more time—and who knew if there would be space for him when the elevator car arrived—he elected to take the stairs instead and ran up the five flights to the maternity floor. When he came hurrying in, doing his best not to breathe heavy, he found Eve sitting on her bed, dressed, with her hands folded in her lap like a school girl attending an old-fashioned parochial school.

Glancing at the clock on the wall, he apologized. "Sorry." It wasn't easy not sounding breathless, but he pulled it off. "Traffic," he tacked on by way of an explanation.

"You really don't have to do this," she told him. "I could have easily asked Vera or Josiah to take us home. Not that I don't appreciate it, but there was no need for you to break up your day like this."

Was she annoyed, or trying to distance herself from him? Either way, he wasn't here to get into a discussion. He was here to make sure she was safe. That was the main reason he was here, he told himself.

Adam quickly scanned the room. Nothing seemed out of place. The flowers he'd brought her yesterday had been transferred into a simple glass vase. The teddy bear was seated not too far from it.

"You have everything?" he asked her.

"I will once the nurse brings Brooklyn."

Adam laughed. "I meant other than that." He looked around again and came to the same conclusion.

"I didn't exactly have time to bring anything, remember?" There hadn't even been the traditional suitcase to grab because, confident that she still had several weeks to go, she hadn't bothered to pack one. So much for living up to the Boy Scout motto.

"Traveling light has its advantages," Adam commented. Moving the teddy bear right next to the flowers on the table, he asked, "What's the protocol? Are we supposed to buzz for the nurse to tell her you're ready to go, or should I go out and see if I can find her instead?"

We. The single, deceptively small word echoed in her head. He made it sound as if they were a unit. A family. But they were nothing of the kind, Eve reminded herself. Adam's sense of responsibility was warmly comforting, but she wasn't fooling herself. Her gut told her that this wasn't going to last. Not unless he'd actually told her the truth. That he meant what he'd said when he claimed to be through with his old way of life. It could happen. It could be true. He could have given his old life up, opting for a clean slate. Maybe this was him, trying to live his life as best he could.

Don't get caught up in a fantasy. You know better.

"I'll try buzzing for her." Eve reached over for the call button.

Very gently, he took the device from her. "I might have more luck," he told her when she looked at him in surprise. Putting the call button aside, Adam stepped out into the hall.

"You probably will," she murmured. She doubted many women could ignore Adam or say no to him.

He was back in less than a minute. She was about to ask if he'd changed his mind, then stopped when she saw that he was not alone. Shadowing Adam was the slender young nurse, Kathy, who had attended to her earlier.

"All set?" Kathy asked cheerfully.

"That I am," Eve assured her. Preparing to get up, she slid to the edge of the bed.

"I'll go get your little princess." The promise, Eve noted, was made not to her, but to Adam.

"She thinks Brooklyn is yours," Eve commented.

Adam's eyes met hers for a long moment. "She is," he reminded her.

After being on her own and thinking of the next eighteen years in terms of just the baby and her, sharing Brooklyn was going to take her a great deal of getting used to—and she wasn't really convinced that it was worth the effort. She'd had enough pain in her life without consciously leaving herself open for more.

But he was the father.

She'd think about it all later, Eve promised herself. For now, she just needed to get home.

"Here she is," Kathy announced, walking in with the swaddled infant.

Hesitating before Adam, the young woman seemed undecided as to whom to give the baby to. A moment later, the nurse opted for the traditional choice. She passed the sleeping infant to Eve.

"Wait right here, I'll bring in the wheelchair," Kathy told her.

"I can walk," Eve protested, calling after the nurse's back.

The young woman returned in a heartbeat, pushing the wheelchair in front of her. She pulled down the brakes on either side of the chair, then took the baby back for a moment, waiting for Eve to get into the wheelchair.

"Hospital policy. I could lose my job if I let you walk out the front door," Kathy told her.

Taking her arm, Adam helped Eve into the wheelchair. "Wouldn't want that."

It wasn't clear to Eve if he was addressing his words to her or to the nurse. Making the best of it, she put her arms out for the baby.

The second the transfer was completed, Brooklyn woke up and began to fuss.

It was happening, Eve thought, banking down the panicky feeling as she gazed down into her daughter's face. Brooklyn and she were on the cusp of starting their new life together.

Nerves undulated throughout her system. All the things she could do wrong with this baby suddenly paraded through her mind.

Her panic intensified. She wasn't ready.

"Don't worry," Adam whispered, lowering his lips to her ear so that only she could hear. "You're going to be great."

How could he possibly have known what she was thinking? Eve twisted around to look at him, a quizzical expression of disbelief on her face. "How did you…?"

The smile he gave her magically restored at least some of her confidence.

"Not so hard to guess what's going through your mind right now," he assured her.

Eve blew out a breath. It was going to be all right, she told herself. It was going to be all right.

If she repeated the sentence a few hundred times, she thought philosophically, she might just wind up convincing herself.

Maybe.

Adam glanced up into the rearview mirror. Again. He'd been doing it with a fair amount of consistency since they'd left the hospital.

He wasn't watching for tailgaters.

The last ten miles to her house, he wasn't certain if his imagination played tricks on him or if his instincts were dead-on. Either way, he could have sworn that a car was tailing him. A late-model domestic beige sedan followed two cars behind his. So far, he'd only managed to get two of the numbers on the license plate.

When he pulled up into Eve's two-car driveway, the beige car passed her house and continued down the street. Was he paranoid or were his survival instincts so finely tuned that he could spot a tail a mile away? Right now, he couldn't answer that with any kind of authority.

After parking his car, Adam quickly got out and rounded the back of the vehicle. He opened the passenger door and extended his hand to Eve.

Rather than resort to bravado, she reluctantly wrapped her fingers around his hand. Trying to get up on her own, she realized that he actually pulled her to her feet. She was still wobbly. So much so that she had to steady herself by grabbing on to his arm.

Surprised, concerned, Adam held her for a moment. "Are you all right?"

"Just a little light-headed," she admitted. "But I'm fine now. You can let go."

He did so, but only slowly, watching her carefully as he withdrew his arms.

She hated feeling like this. How had women managed to give birth and then continue working in the fields decades ago?

Turning carefully, she looked into the backseat. Brooklyn was strapped securely in an infant seat. An infant seat Adam had bought because she hadn't gotten around to it. Again, because she'd felt she still had a few weeks left in which to prepare.

"By the way, how much do I owe you?"

About to open the rear passenger door, he stopped and looked at her. "For what?" he asked incredulously. "For the ride home?"

"No, for the infant seat." She felt remiss in being caught so unprepared. But then, this whole pregnancy had caught her unprepared. "I was going to pick one up this weekend."

"And now you have one," he told her. "You don't owe me anything, Eve. The baby's half-mine, remember?"

Her mouth curved in amusement. "Which half are you claiming?"

"It's too early to tell," he quipped. "I'll get back to you on that."

After removing the belts from around his daughter, he picked her up and then gently tucked the baby into the crook of his arm as if he'd been doing this all his life. There was no need for Eve to know that he had bought a life-size baby doll at the toy store and had been practicing this since yesterday.

Adam slipped his free hand around her waist, ready to help guide her up the front walk. "Okay, let's get you both into the house."

The short distance seemed to stretch out before her like a twenty-mile run. Pressing her lips together, Eve walked up the path on shaky legs. She surrendered her key to Adam and waited for him to unlock the door. Once inside, she headed toward the sofa, relieved to be able to rest.

As she sank down on the sofa, she could feel Adam watching her. She hated letting him see her like this. It wasn't part of her self-image.

"This is just temporary," she assured him.

He shifted Brooklyn to his other side. "No reason to believe it's not," he agreed.

Under the pretext of closing the door, he looked out and saw the car he'd thought was tailing them pass by in the opposite direction. It was quite possible that the driver was lost, looking for an address in an unfamiliar neighborhood. But he hadn't lived this long in a dangerous field by being lax. He remained on his guard. The stakes were higher now than they had ever been.

Crossing to the sofa, he laid the baby down in the bassinette that stood beside the sofa. He'd purchased the item yesterday when he'd gone to get the infant seat.

"Look, I have to get back to the shop for a little while." Sederholm was going to call him this afternoon and he didn't want to have to take the phone call around her. "But I'll be back later."

He had already done more than enough. She needed to process things, to find a way to get used to dealing with all this—without becoming used to having him around.

"You don't—"

"—have to," he completed the sentence for her, banking down a wave of impatience. "Yes, I know. But you're obviously not yourself yet, and taking care of a newborn isn't a walk in the park." He remembered how exhausted his mother had been when his baby sister was first born. "It's demanding. So, unless you have some kind of support system in place, I'll be hanging around for a week or so until you can get on your feet again."

"A week?" she echoed.

"Or so," he added again.

"Or so," she whispered in disbelief.

She knew her hormones were in flux and she could always blame this roller-coaster ride on them. But right at this moment, sitting in the shade of Adam's unexpected offer, Eve wasn't sure if she wanted to laugh—or cry.

Chapter 8

"What's this?"

The question Eve asked pertained to the eight-by-eleven manila envelope Adam had handed her on his way to the kitchen.

Having taken care of business both at New Again, the rare first-edition bookstore in Newport Beach he supposedly owned, and with Sederholm, the latter involving humoring the college student, Adam had made a quick stop to pick up dinner for Eve and himself. He'd gone to an actual Mexican restaurant that had takeout on the side, rather than going to one of the numerous fast-food places that touted familiar Mexican meals. Time might be at a premium, but taste didn't necessarily have to suffer because of it.

"Dinner," he answered, assuming that she was asking

about the two large white bags he carried into the kitchen. Adam turned to look at her over his shoulder as he deposited the bags on the counter. "Don't worry, I made sure your portion wasn't too spicy, in case you're—you know." His voice trailed off as he avoided her eyes.

Considering the incredibly intimate contact they'd already shared, not just when they'd made love months ago, but during the far more recent process of bringing their daughter into the world, Eve found it strangely amusing and perhaps more than a little touching and sweet that Adam had turned suddenly shy.

"Well, just for the record, I am 'you knowing,'" she told him, making no attempt to hide her smile at his polite reference to her breastfeeding, "so that was very thoughtful of you, but I was actually referring to this." She held up the manila envelope. "What is it?" she asked again.

His back to her, Adam began to take their dinners out of the bags and placed the various wrapped selections on the granite counter. "Insurance."

She glanced back at the envelope, not sure if she even wanted to open the clasp and peer inside. "Against what?" she asked slowly.

"No, insurance," he repeated, turning around. She was still holding the envelope in her hands. Most women would have already ripped it open. That made her incredibly devoid of curiosity, he thought. "*Life* insurance," he emphasized, adding, "on me," when her expression remained bewildered.

Eve turned the envelope over in her hands, regarding it the way someone might a brand-new alien lifeform—and finding it displeasing.

"Okay. Again, why?" This was completely out of the blue and it made her feel uncomfortable without really understanding why. "Is there something wrong with you?" Even as she asked, the dark suspicion behind the words hit her. "You're not going to…?"

"Die?" he supplied with a touch of amusement. "Well, I'm not planning on it, but you never know." Especially considering his real line of work and the kinds of people he found himself dealing with on almost a regular basis. "And *if* something should happen to me, I want to make sure that Brooklyn's taken care of." He'd almost included her in the statement, but his gut told him that she would balk at that. He had more of a chance of her going along with this if she thought only the baby was named as a beneficiary.

Not that she seemed exactly thrilled with this revised version, either.

The expression that came over her face was like a dark storm rolling over the prairie, swallowing the terrain whole.

"What's the matter?" he prodded. "I'm just doing the responsible thing," he added when Eve didn't answer his question.

It hit her then. She knew why he was doing this. If he had really become a responsible person, he would have abandoned the life that had initially caused their separation.

"You're still involved, aren't you?" The evenly worded accusation was the only conclusion she could draw. Men his age didn't ordinarily think about death— unless they dealt with people who could make that sort of thing a reality. "In the drug world," she emphasized when he raised his eyebrows quizzically. She wasn't taken in by his act. "You didn't quit dealing," she cried angrily. "You *lied* to me," she accused, lightning all but flashing from her eyes. How stupid could she have been, believing him when he'd told her dealing was all in his past and he was here for a fresh start without the old ties.

Lies had always come easily to him. He considered them a necessary defense mechanism that he had to use in order to remain alive. What was lying but another form of pretense? Actors "lied" all the time when they assumed a role, pretending to be someone else on the screen or on the stage.

He was merely being a good, convincing actor, that's all.

But lying to this woman who had borne his child, who had managed to turn his world upside down, that was something else again. For reasons he didn't have time to fully explore, he found it difficult to continue deceiving her.

However, he had no choice. Far more people were involved than just him. Consequently, it wasn't entirely his secret to share.

So he twisted around her words. "Are you going to stand there and tell me that everyone who has a life insurance policy is a drug dealer?"

"No, but—"

"But I am, is that it?" His voice was low, quietly echoing barely controlled anger. Adam borrowed a few facts from his life, augmenting them to suit the occasion. "I originally took out this policy so that if anything happened to me, Mona, my kid sister, would be able to take care of herself." Mentioning his sister, even in passing, brought a wave of irate sadness to him. "Mona was never much good at hanging on to a job. I just wanted to be sure she'd be okay."

Then why had he given this to her for Brooklyn? She didn't have to open the envelope to know that he had obviously changed the designated beneficiary. "Where is your sister now?" she asked. An uneasy feeling slipped over her the moment the words were out of her mouth.

She saw his jaw clench. "She died."

"Oh." Sympathy flooded her. She knew what it was like to lose someone. More than one someone. "I'm sorry." Eve bit her lower lip. "What did your sister die of?"

"It doesn't matter. She's dead," he said with such dark finality, Eve felt as if she'd literally been pushed away. He began opening the top drawers that ran along the underside of the counter, looking for utensils. "I changed the beneficiary. The policy's in trust for Brooklyn until she turns twenty-one." He spared her a glance. "Until then, if the occasion arises, you manage it for her." He nodded toward the envelope. "Put that in a safe place."

She stared at the envelope, then shook her head as she pushed it toward him on the counter. "I don't want it."

"It isn't for you," he pointed out. "It's for Brooklyn."

He watched as she squared her shoulders like a soldier being challenged. "I can take care of my daughter—"

His eyes held hers. "*Our* daughter," Adam corrected pointedly.

She just couldn't figure him out, not on any level.

Here was an intelligent man who could have been anything, yet he had sunk down to the level of a drug dealer. Was perhaps still at the level.

"Most men would fight this tooth and nail," she said quietly. "Or at least insist on a paternity test, yet you're willing to accept that you're Brooklyn's father without any tangible proof."

Adam saw nothing wrong with that. Finally finding the utensils, he took out two knives and two forks, placing them on the counter. He pushed the envelope back in her direction.

"So?"

"So why aren't you asking for proof? A DNA test? Why are you taking just my word for it?"

"Maybe because you *didn't* ask me for anything." And then he shrugged. "The timing just works out." His eyes dipped down to her stomach. Even now, she seemed to be well on her way to regaining her figure— which, as he recalled, had been drop-dead gorgeous. "Besides," he raised his eyes to her face, eyeing her knowingly, "you're not the kind to have casual sex."

"How do you know that?" she challenged. Granted she'd been a virgin when they'd made love, but they hadn't been together long enough for him to have drawn this kind of a hard and fast conclusion. "What makes you think you know so much about me?"

His smile went straight to her gut.

Adam shrugged carelessly. "I just know. Call it a gut feeling."

It was more than just his gut that was involved, although that had been the initial proponent. When he'd received that e-mail that had sent him looking for Eve, he'd gotten Spenser at the department to do a little research for him. The reformed computer hacker put together a file that contained a great deal of information on the woman standing beside him.

Adam handed her a plate. "Now stop being stubborn and have something to eat before—"

As if on cue, the baby monitor on the counter came to life. Something that sounded very close to mewling filled the room.

"The baby cries?" she guessed, ending his sentence for him.

He nodded, then murmured, "Too late." He glanced over his shoulder, although there was no way he could see Brooklyn's room. "Eat," he told Eve, indicating her plate and the selection of entrees. "If you tell me which way to her bedroom, I'll go see what Her Majesty wants."

The aroma of the still-hot food caused her stomach to contract and growl. The spread before her proved to be too much of a temptation.

"It's upstairs," she told him. "Second room on your right."

She watched as Adam walked out of the kitchen. With all her heart, she wished she could banish her lingering suspicions about him. If it weren't for her nagging doubts, she would admit he was damn near perfect in this new paternal role.

He was rising to the occasion far better than she was, Eve thought, helping herself to a corn-husk-wrapped tamale. Though she dearly loved this brand-new addition in her life, a part of her was still afraid she was going to wind up being a very poor mother.

* * *

When Adam didn't return within a few minutes, carrying a hungry baby in his arms, Eve began to wonder what was taking him so long. Only one way to find out. Bracing her hands on the counter, she slid off the stool and went to investigate.

Although she wanted to hurry up the stairs, she forced herself to take it slow. It annoyed her no end that she still felt pretty weak. The last nap the baby had taken, she'd taken one, too. Filled with admiration for mothers who continued to be powerhouses, Eve couldn't wait to be her old self again.

Walking into the baby's room, she saw that Adam was at the changing table—one of the gifts Josiah had given the baby that she *had* accepted—putting the finishing touches on the disposable diaper he'd just secured around Brooklyn's tiny bottom.

He sensed rather than heard or saw Eve in the doorway. "She needed changing."

She crossed to him. "You change diapers?" she asked incredulously.

He'd changed more than his share of Mona's diapers. The knack was something akin to riding a bicycle. You never really forgot how—especially when plastic tabs were involved.

"It's not exactly like changing water into wine," he pointed out, glancing at her awed expression. "Anyone can do it if they need to." Picking his daughter up off the changing table, he smoothed down her tiny dress and turned around to look at Eve. "There, I think we'll all be a little more comfortable having her dirty diaper a thing of the past."

Who would have thought he'd take to parenting better than she did? "You are full of surprises, Adam Smythe." She didn't bother to hide the admiration in her voice.

They were sharing a moment. It took a great deal of self-control not to tell her that his name wasn't Smythe, but Serrano. But Adam managed to hold his piece and only commented, "You'd be surprised," making certain that the proper smile was on his lips.

Not entirely. The stray thought popped up in her head, taunting her. She banked it down, refusing to let it bring her down. The man was trying, that was all that mattered.

Taking the baby from him, she pointed toward the hall and the stairs that were beyond. "I'd better feed her. You go ahead and have dinner. Brooklyn and I'll be along as soon as she's finished."

"You know, if you prepare a few bottles ahead of time, we could take turns feeding her," he suggested, turning from the doorway.

Eve was already sitting in the rocking chair holding Brooklyn to her breast. The infant eagerly suckled as if she hadn't been fed for days instead of a little less than four hours ago.

Adam's breath caught in his throat. He couldn't remember when he'd ever seen anything even remotely as beautiful.

Belatedly, he realized he was staring. Clearing his throat, he abruptly looked away, even though he would have been content just to stand there, watching the scene all evening.

"I'll wait for you in the kitchen," he murmured to the bedroom door just before he left the room.

Eve smiled to herself. Again, his actions surprised

her. Adam Smythe was a very complex individual, with a lot of different layers. And she was getting a lot of mixed signals here. How did she tell them apart? Just what was real and what was imagined?

More than anything, she wished she knew what to believe and just who and what Adam Smythe really was. But she didn't see that happening anytime soon. And who knew? He might be gone tomorrow.

She tried to prepare herself, secretly hoping that tomorrow wouldn't come for a very long time.

Within a week, they fell into a routine, one that Adam was loathe to give up or even change in the slightest manner. Every night he would come home to her, to them, and share both the responsibilities and the rewards of caring for Brooklyn. And for what it was worth, all three of them seemed to be thriving.

The weather had even cooperated, in a manner of speaking. An unexpected storm off the coast of Colombia had sent residents along the coast scrambling for their lives. More importantly, at least for Adam, was that the shipment of drugs loaded into the belly of an airplane bound for California had been lost when the plane suddenly went down.

With great bravado, Daniel Sederholm had insisted that another shipment could be on its way as quickly as within ten days. Though the setback had his handler's teeth on edge, Adam had ten more days to enjoy this secret life he'd miraculously stumbled into. Ten more days to pretend that the world wouldn't come knocking on his door, dragging him away at a moment's notice.

Ten more days to watch his daughter grow and have

both Brooklyn and her mother burrow their way even further into his heart.

As if they hadn't deeply entrenched themselves there already.

"So I take it that he's moved in?" Josiah asked Eve.

It was midafternoon and her self-appointed guardian angel had come by for a visit. Outside, his driver, Lucas, sat in his restored classic Mercedes, engrossed in the latest page-turner put out by the current darling of the bestseller list. Meanwhile, Josiah sat in Eve's living room, quietly studying the young woman he regarded as another daughter over the rim of his teacup. Fragrant vanilla-flavored coffee wafted up to penetrate his senses, soothing him. He was flattered that she kept his coffee of choice on hand for his visits.

For his part, he'd been as patient as he could, giving Eve almost two weeks to settle into a routine before finally inviting himself over to see how she was doing. It had taken him exactly five minutes to deduce that his favorite veterinarian wasn't tackling parenthood alone.

"Adam's here temporarily," Eve was quick to correct. Having poured herself a cup, as well, she sat down opposite Josiah.

"And you're all right with that?" Josiah cocked his head slightly, as if that could help him assess the situation more clearly.

"I am."

His eyes seemed to delve into hers, as if accessing her very thoughts. "You don't mind that he plans to leave after a finite point?"

"Oh." She'd thought Josiah was asking her how she

was dealing with having Adam around, not if she minded the fact that he intended to leave in the near future. "To be honest, this is all still a little overwhelming for me. I'm not really thinking more than a few hours ahead at a time."

He nodded. Whether she knew it or not, that was what she had him for. He had always been good at looking at the big picture. His former line of work called for it. Josiah moved forward on the sofa, creating a more intimate atmosphere. "How much do you know about this man, Eve?"

"I know he's a good man." The moment the words were out of her mouth, she realized that she sounded defensive. She didn't want to be defensive and hoped Josiah would come to the right conclusion about Adam on his own. "He gave me his life insurance policy to hang on to for safekeeping. He named Brooklyn as his beneficiary."

Josiah nodded slowly, absorbing the information. "Admirable."

The word was polite, detached. "You don't like him, do you?"

Because he knew he couldn't say what she wanted to hear, Josiah avoided giving her a direct answer. "I'm not the one who counts here, Eve. And I'm just worried about you," he admitted. "And, I suppose, I'm worried about myself, as well."

Her eyebrows drew together into a puzzled line. "I don't follow."

"Well, if this Adam hurts you again—the way he did the last time," Josiah emphasized, "I will be forced to have to kill him, and truthfully, the prospect of 'doing time' at my age is not exactly pleasant."

Setting down her cup on the coffee table, Eve laughed. She leaned forward and placed her hand on his shoulder. "You won't have to kill him, Josiah. He's really nicer than you think."

Thin, aristocratic shoulders rose and fell in a careless shrug. "What I think doesn't matter."

"What you think matters to me, Josiah," she assured him. "You've always been like an uncle to me. If Adam does become a permanent part of my life," she went on, constructing her sentences carefully, "I'd want the two of you to get along." She abruptly remembered the holiday that was coming up. She really was living in a fog these days, Eve thought ruefully. "Tell you what. Thanksgiving is almost here. Why don't you come over to my house for dinner and maybe, properly wined and dined, the two of you can do a little more than just try to stare each other down."

Josiah looked at her, aghast. "But you can't cook, Eve."

"Why can't I?" she asked, confused. She'd cooked for him before. Was he blurting out what he really thought of her efforts? She'd always thought of herself as a good cook. "I've been doing it since I was ten."

"No, no, I mean, you just gave birth. Cooking is taxing, especially a big meal like Thanksgiving. You shouldn't exert yourself."

"By Thanksgiving it'll be closer to four weeks than to 'just,'" she pointed out, smiling at his concern. "And as for not exerting myself, I solemnly promise I won't go hunting for the turkey anywhere but the grocery store this year."

Josiah sighed. He knew it was useless to argue. Eve

had been a stubborn little girl and she had grown up to be a stubborn young woman. When she made up her mind about something, no one could talk her out of it. It was both a source of pride and despair for her father, Josiah recalled.

"You are a hard young woman to keep down, Eve Walters."

She smiled warmly at him. "So I've been told. Then it's settled? You'll come?"

"Yes, I will come. As long as you allow me to bring dessert."

Pleased, Eve put out her hand. He took it in his bony one and shook it. "Done," she told him. Just then, a lusty wail was heard over the baby monitor positioned on the coffee table. "Ah, I believe that's Brooklyn asking to see her great-uncle."

He rose to his feet, remarkably agile for a man in the latter half of his life. "Then let's not disappoint her." With a flourish, he bowed at the waist and offered the crook of his arm to her.

Rising, Eve hooked her arm through his. "Let's not," she agreed with a warm smile.

Chapter 9

It looked as if a tornado had made a pit stop in her kitchen, leaving pots, measuring spoons and cups, and ingredients—both large and small—scattered every which way.

At the moment, Eve felt just a shade away from overwhelmed. She scanned the formerly neat kitchen and sighed. The clock on the wall to her immediate right kept insisting on swallowing up minutes. She was running out of time and falling drastically behind.

Though she hated to admit it, Eve realized she'd bitten off a little more than she could chew. Okay, a lot more. She was seriously regretting having turned down Adam's offer. He'd volunteered to bring a fully cooked turkey dinner, prepared by a local caterer, to the table for her. At the time, she'd turned him down, confident that she could pull it off the way she had before.

Thanks to Adam's help every evening, she'd been getting more sleep and grew stronger. So much so that she thought, since it was nearly a month since she'd given birth to Brooklyn, she finally was back to her old self.

But standing here, in the middle of her chaotic kitchen, with the stuffing only half-baked and demanding her attention, the potatoes refusing for some unknown reason to cook to the point where they were soft enough to mash, and the turkey needing basting every fifteen minutes, not to mention that she had to stop periodically to feed or change an overly fussy baby, her goal of having everything ready by five o'clock was becoming the impossible dream.

Sound suddenly emanated from the baby monitor on the counter. Brooklyn was awake and crying. Again.

Eve pressed her lips together, trying to ignore the sound.

Brooklyn's wail grew louder.

Her daughter had gotten accustomed to being scooped up within moments of voicing her displeasure. Eve knew schools of child-rearing sometimes frowned on that, claiming that to deny instant gratification was actually good for the baby. But the sound of her baby's cries just twisted her heart. Besides, she reasoned, how could too much love be a bad thing?

Still, today would have been a good day to put one of those "let the baby cry a little" theories to the test. Eve tried and remained where she was.

She lasted all of a minute and a half. Throwing up

her hands, she wiped them on her apron then hurried to the staircase.

"Mama's coming," she called out, taking the stairs as quickly as she could.

The pitiful cries continued until she entered Brooklyn's room.

"Maybe you'd like to come down and give me a few pointers," she said to her daughter as she picked the infant up.

Brooklyn sighed deeply, as if some horrible wrong had just been righted, then lay her head down on her mother's shoulder, tucking herself against her mother's neck.

The missing piece of my puzzle, Eve thought, patting the baby's bottom. She could almost feel the deep affection in her chest doubling the moment Brooklyn lay her head down.

Remaining where she was for a moment, Eve drew in a deep breath. No offensive odor registered. "Okay, you don't need changing and you just ate an hour ago, so you're not hungry. You're just lonely up here, aren't you?" she murmured, stroking her daughter's back. It was a toss up who was more soothed by the action, Eve mused, Brooklyn or her. "Okay, come with me," she said cheerfully, leaving the room and heading for the stairs. "I know just where to put you."

On his last visit—yesterday—Josiah had brought yet another gift for the baby. It was what amounted to a motorized port-a-crib, complete with music some expert declared that babies enjoyed. He'd had Lucas put it together for her. The finished product currently stood in the family room.

"Time to put this little contraption to the test," Eve announced. Very carefully, she deposited Brooklyn into the port-a-crib.

The moment her back made contact with the thin mattress on the bottom of the crib, Brooklyn began to fuss again. Eve quickly wound the motor. The port-a-crib slowly swayed to and fro, the gentle action keeping time with the soft strains of a lullaby.

Brooklyn's eyes widened. Entranced, she stopped crying. Her expression became alert, as if trying to pinpoint where the sound came from.

If she didn't know better, Eve thought, she would have said her daughter was smiling.

"Bless you, Josiah," Eve murmured. With slow, careful movements, she repositioned the port-a-crib so that she could easily keep an eye on it from the kitchen.

Eve had no sooner done that than a loud hissing noise demanded her attention. The water in the pot with the potatoes had finally begun to boil, and just like that, it was boiling over. The water splashed onto the surface of the electric burner and cascaded down along the front of the stove.

The last time that had happened, Eve suddenly remembered, the stove had short-circuited, throwing the oven portion out of commission for an entire day. She didn't have an entire day to spare. She didn't even have half an hour to spare, she thought, trying to bank down a wave of panic.

"No, no, no," Eve cried, as if the urgent entreaty could somehow perform a miracle and send the water retreating like the Red Sea scene in the classic *The Ten Commandments*.

Grabbing a towel, Eve frantically stemmed the descending tide. In the background, she heard the doorbell ring.

Now what?

It was too early for either Adam or Josiah and his driver to arrive. People didn't sell magazines door-to-door around here on Thanksgiving, did they?

She decided to ignore whoever was on the other side of the door. But the doorbell rang a second time. And Tessa, suddenly alert, began to run back and forth from the front door to the kitchen.

Now someone was knocking instead of ringing. She glanced at her dog as she made a second round-trip dash. "What is it, Lassie? Did Timmy fall into the well?"

Tessa barked, as if in response to the question.

Feeling harried, Eve looked over toward Brooklyn to make sure everything was all right, then hurried over to the front door.

She pulled it open without bothering to ask who it was. If it was a serial killer, the dog would protect her. Or so she hoped.

It wasn't a serial killer. It was Adam. Early.

"Didn't I give you a key?" she asked him, an irritated note threatening her voice. Her dog, apparently, was overjoyed at the early appearance and behaved as if she hadn't seen him for months instead of a handful of hours.

Turning on her heel, Eve quickly returned to the scene of her pending disaster.

The scent of scorched surfaces and burned water faintly teased his nose as Adam followed her to the kitchen. Things weren't going too well, he noticed, but wisely kept the observation to himself.

"Yes, but that's only for emergencies, like if I think you've passed out and hit your head on something. Otherwise, I didn't think you would want me just waltzing in."

Thinking back, she realized that she had let him in each time. "You practically live here these days." The only time he left was to go to work or get a change of clothes. That pretty much constituted him living with her. "Having you let yourself in wouldn't have upset some delicate balance of power," she assured him.

Pausing to pet the dog, Adam then went directly to the port-a-crib. Brooklyn began gurgling and kicking her feet. Her big blue eyes appeared focused on Adam.

Hardly a month old and she was already a flirt, Eve thought with a shake of her head.

"Hi, short stuff," Adam teased, tickling the baby's belly.

The sound of Brooklyn's delighted laughter filled the air, warming Eve's heart.

Walking away from the crib, Adam crossed back to the kitchen. His eyes swept around the room. Keeping a straight face, he asked Eve, "Need help?"

"No." The word came out like a warning shot fired at a potential intruder. "I've got everything under control here."

Rather than dispute her claim, Adam slid onto the closest stool. Propping his upturned palm beneath his chin, he just stared unabashedly at her.

"What are you doing?" she demanded.

"Waiting for your nose to grow," he replied simply.

"Happened in a fairy tale. Little wooden boy lied, his nose grew something awful."

She held up her hand to stop him from going on. "I am aware of the fairy tale," she informed him through gritted teeth, "and I am *not* lying."

He gave her a knowing look, pretending to humor her. "Lucky for you, fairy tales don't come true." He slid off the stool and looked around. Enough was enough. It was time to get down to business. "All right, where do you want me to get started?"

She gave up the protest with a heartfelt sigh. "Do you have a magic wand?"

He laughed. "I don't think you need that much help. Just a little," he added, trying to bolster her morale. "Why don't we divide up the work? Would that make things easier on you?"

"I used to be able to handle everything," she told him with an air of helplessness.

The water in the pot finally simmered down, sinking to its new level. A lot of water had gone over the side. Wanting to replenish what was lost, she grabbed the pot by its handles in order to refill it and immediately yelped, releasing the pot again. Why she'd suddenly forgotten that there was no coating on the pot handles was completely beyond her.

Grabbing her hands in his, Adam quickly moved her toward the sink. He turned the faucet on and ran cold water over her palms.

What was wrong with her? She knew to do that, to instantly apply cold to the affected area in order to minimize the damage. Had giving birth completely diminished her brain power?

"And you'll be able to handle everything again— soon," Adam promised her, still holding her hands beneath the running water. "But for now, there's nothing wrong with accepting a little help when you're not firing on all four cylinders," he added mildly. Releasing her hands, he reached for a towel and offered it to her. "Why don't I take over the mashed potatoes—I am assuming they're going to be mashed." He looked at her, waiting for confirmation.

She bit back a wince as she wiped the towel over her tender fingers. "Yes, they're going to be mashed."

He regarded the potatoes for a moment, then raised his eyes to meet hers. "You make them with garlic, parmesan and mozzarella cheeses and milk?"

"That was the plan, more or less." She wouldn't have thought of adding the cheeses, but that did sound good.

"Great." He reached for the whisk she kept housed in a colorful jar on the counter, along with several other utensils. "I can take out all my aggression on the potatoes."

Opening the refrigerator to take out the one dessert she'd prepared last night, Eve stopped to give him a puzzled look. "What aggression?"

"Just a little joke," Adam assured her as he moved over to the sink and, using pot holders, drained the potatoes. A cloud of steam rose, but he deftly avoided coming in contact with it, drawing back his head. "Apparently very little," he commented more to himself than to her.

"I'm sorry, but you've thrown me off by coming now. I didn't expect you until later," she told him, then turned her attention to the stuffing she'd placed in the oven earlier.

Opening the top oven, she raised the aluminum foil

away from the rectangular pan, wanting to reassure herself that nothing was burning. This represented three-quarters of the stuffing. The remaining quarter was inside the turkey, absorbing the bird's juices for added flavor. She would make sure that Adam sampled it. She wasn't quite sure why she was so set on showing him she was a good cook, but in the last few minutes, it had become very important to her.

"Sorry, I didn't mean to throw you off," he apologized. "But the store's closed today and I had nothing to do. I don't like having a lot of time on my hands."

That much was true. There'd been a quick touching of bases with not only his handler—who was on his way to spend the holiday with his sister and her family—but with Sederholm, as well. He'd gone to see Sederholm to find out firsthand how things were coming along with the replacement shipment. He'd had to listen to the cocky college senior delineate his getaway plan, the one he intended to use on his parents by skipping out on the evening meal. Sederholm had sounded more than a little paranoid as he assured him that everything was on schedule and that he'd have his supply "soon."

Once he'd gotten all that out of the way, Adam caught himself thinking about Eve. Constantly. That very fact should have thrown up all sorts of red flags for him. He should be trying to stay away from her. It just wasn't working out for him. Being away from Eve only made him want to see her more. The trite saying was right. Absence, even absence involving a mere matter of hours, made the heart grow fonder.

Adam sighed. He was becoming entrenched in this

"helpful lover" role he'd taken on. So much so that it was taking center stage with him. He knew the danger. It made him let his guard down, interfered with his focus. Which in turn endangered not just him and the people he worked with, but Eve and Brooklyn, as well.

He couldn't allow anything to happen to them.

Maybe they'd all be better off if he just walked away.

Damned if he did and damned if he didn't. What was the right call? He honestly wasn't sure.

Tomorrow. He'd think about that and make up his mind tomorrow. Today, there were different priorities to consider.

"So I thought I'd come over and see if I could lend you a hand or at least some support," he continued. "My mother used to say that I was pretty handy in the kitchen."

"Your mother?" she echoed. He didn't strike her as the type to talk about his mother. She didn't think of him as warm and fuzzy.

"You sound surprised." Adam grinned, amused. "Even I had parents."

"I didn't mean to imply that I thought you didn't, but you don't exactly talk about your family."

Adam forced his voice to sound light, as if the subject and what had happened hadn't been carved into his heart.

"There's a reason for that."

Was it her imagination, or was he working that whisk particularly hard? He really *was* taking out his feelings on the potatoes. "And that is?"

"I don't have a family," he told her simply. "Not anymore."

He'd told her that his sister was dead, but he hadn't mentioned anything about his parents. She felt instant empathy in her soul. "Your parents are dead?"

"Yes."

The single word was completely devoid of any feeling, any telltale indications of the boy who had once been cut to the quick at the sudden deprivation. He hadn't had time to grieve. He had a sister to take care of and a life to carve out for both of them.

Eve turned away from the oven and toward him. "I guess that gives us something in common. I'm an orphan, too."

It felt odd to phrase it that way, because, after all, she was an adult and had felt like one for a very long time now. But the realization that there was no one to fuss over her, to wonder trivial things such as was she eating right and keeping warm, that occasionally made her feel detached from the world at large.

Adam looked into her eyes. It felt as if he delved into her very soul. "I know exactly what you mean," he affirmed softly.

Eve shifted restlessly. She felt herself reacting, not just to the words, but to him. To his very male presence within this, her female-dominated home. It seemed incredible that he still had that effect on her. Knowing what she knew about him, feeling as if he'd betrayed her, at least that initial time, she was still incredibly and irresistibly drawn to him.

She wanted to be with him. And not just with a table between them, but biblically, in the full sense of the word.

Out of the blue she remembered that she'd gone to see her doctor yesterday for her postpartum checkup.

After it was over, Dr. Mudd had expressed surprise at how quickly she'd healed and how fast her body seemed to have bounced back to its prepregnancy form.

When Dr. Mudd had told her that she was "good to go" in all aspects of the concept and could even begin contemplating giving Brooklyn a little brother or sister, Eve had felt herself going pale. Very politely, she'd informed her doctor that she had no intentions of going that route for a very long time to come. Maybe never.

Dr. Mudd had merely given her a knowing look and said the choice, as always, was up to her, but that she'd felt she had to tell her that she could have "relations" if she wanted to.

As if she wanted to, Eve had silently scoffed at the time.

But the problem was that whenever Adam was around, she found herself wanting to.

A lot.

Why was she thinking about this? Heaven knew she had more than enough to deal with right now and Vera was dying to have her finally return to the practice. She made plans to that end, thinking that she would get started next Monday. Between the baby and her career, she had more than enough in her life to keep her occupied. She certainly didn't need to complicate things even further by inviting a man into her life.

Into their lives, she amended. Because what affected her affected Brooklyn. They were a set now. The fact that the man she was contemplating—fleetingly—to allow into her life was Brooklyn's father didn't change anything. Hell, he was the reason she was feeling this edginess in the first place.

At bottom, despite the fact that he did pitch in on all

levels to help her cope with the changes in her life, and more specifically, to help her take care of the baby, she still couldn't bring herself to fully trust him or be able to take him at his word.

No matter how much she wanted to.

Chapter 10

"This has to be, by far, the best Thanksgiving turkey I've ever eaten," Lucas told Eve as he consumed the last bite of his dinner. Josiah's tall, muscular driver had the uncanny ability to appear both enthusiastic and quiet at the same time.

At first, when Eve had extended the invitation to join them at the table, the man had demurred, assuring her that he was fine with waiting for Josiah in the car. He'd held up the mystery he was currently reading and said that he would have an instrumental CD playing on the Mercedes's sound system.

When she'd pressed him as to what he intended to eat while they were inside, consuming a turkey dinner with all the trimmings, he'd produced a couple of those breakfast energy bars that boasted of having chocolate and raspberries in its mix.

Shaking her head, Eve had confiscated the bars, telling him that there was no way he was going to sit in her driveway gnawing on hardened granola, especially not on Thanksgiving.

Observing the exchange, Josiah had chuckled drily. "I wouldn't argue with her if I were you, Lucas," he'd told his driver. "I know for a fact that Dr. Eve can be a very stubborn young woman when she wants to be."

Listening, Adam had laughed. "Now there's an understatement if I've ever heard one. But he's right, you know," he went on to tell Josiah's driver. "She's going to keep after you until you give up. Might as well not let the turkey get cold and just give in."

He didn't appear to be the type who liked stirring things up. Lucas capitulated. Coming inside, he'd sat down at the dining-room table, taking a seat next to Josiah. When presented with the meal, he had eaten with gusto, consuming a great deal more than the man he had been chauffeuring around, plus the other two people at the table, as well.

Retiring his utensils, Josiah delicately wiped his mouth and added his voice to the praise. "Yes." He smiled at Eve warmly. "My compliments to the chef."

"Thank you," she replied, more than a little pleased. "But I really can't take all the credit," she protested in the next breath. "Dinner wouldn't have been ready at all if Adam hadn't helped."

His words belied the intense look in his eyes as Josiah regarded Eve's "helper." "Well, then it was an excellent collaboration. I highly approve." He patted what was still a very flat stomach. "I'm afraid that I am too full to move."

"Then stay. Stay as long as you like," she encouraged. She looked at Lucas. Her invitation was to both men. "I give you my word, no one's going to chase you out."

As she spoke, she rose to her feet and reached for Josiah's plate, intent on clearing away the dishes. Lucas was on his feet immediately. For a large man, he moved with impressive agility. He took the dish away from her and began piling the other plates on top of it.

"The least I can do after that fantastic meal is to clear the table for you and do the dishes," Lucas told her.

"Dishes don't need doing, Lucas. That's why God created dishwashers," she answered.

"Well, I can at least get them from here to there," he told her, piling the utensils on the top dish.

Beneath that polite exterior, she had a feeling that Lucas was as quietly determined to do the right thing as she was. She gave up trying to dissuade him.

Inclining her head, she politely accepted his offer. "Thank you."

Josiah took advantage to the temporary break in the conversation. He leaned forward, his eyes on Adam's. "So tell me, Adam, if you don't mind my asking, how do you like doing business down here?"

The man wasn't mildly curious, he was digging, Adam thought. Why?

"I like it," he said casually, as if he wasn't aware that the older man was placing him under a microscope. "The weather's nicer down here, the people friendlier."

"I see."

Ordinarily, he would have attributed Josiah's fishing to his needing to act as Eve's surrogate father. But something about the way the other man looked at him made Adam rethink this simple conclusion. Maybe the job was really getting him paranoid.

"Is there much money in bookstores these days?" Josiah asked.

"There is in the kinds of books Adam deals in," Eve told the older man. Something unnamed and protective had risen up inside of her.

As if Adam needed protectors, she quietly jeered.

"Still dealing in rare first editions, then?" Josiah asked, his eyebrows raised in query.

"Yes."

"And how is that done, exactly? Where do you find these treasures?" Josiah wanted to know.

Definitely grilling him, Adam thought. "I go to estate sales. You'd be surprised what you can find if you look hard enough," Adam replied.

"I'm sure I would be," Josiah agreed thoughtfully. He glanced toward the kitchen where Lucas was rinsing off plates and stacking them into the dishwasher. "My driver has an affinity for murder-mystery books. Would you by any chance have a first edition of an Agatha Christie book?" he asked, then became more specific in his choice. *"The Mousetrap."*

Adam chuckled. He had just had a mousetrap set for him. Lucky thing he had minored in English in college while working on his degree in criminology.

"The Mousetrap," he informed Josiah needlessly, "was a play, not a book."

The older man seemed properly embarrassed. "Ah, my error." His expression slowly turned hopeful. "Perhaps one of her other efforts?"

As it turned out, he actually had something to sell to Josiah—if the man wanted to continue with the charade. "I have *The Man in the Brown Suit.*"

"Excellent," Josiah declared with just the right amount of enthusiasm. "If you give me the address to your shop, I'll make a point of stopping by next Wednesday. Christmas is coming, you know."

"It usually does after Thanksgiving," Adam commented drily. He reached into his pocket and took out his wallet. In the interest of maintaining his cover, he carried several business cards with him at all times and offered one to the other man.

Taking the card, Josiah studied it for a moment before tucking it into his own pocket. "Next Wednesday," he repeated.

"I'll be looking forward to it," Adam told him.

The old man was up to something. He would bet his last dollar on it. But what? That was the part that didn't make sense. Could it just be that the man was looking out for Eve? Or was there something else involved?

He'd been at this too long, Adam thought darkly. Being undercover for two years had a way of getting to a man. Now a rose was no longer a rose, but could very well be an elaborate listening device.

He missed the days of roses.

"Anyone for dessert?" Eve offered. But just as she rose to her feet, Brooklyn made a low announcement, letting it be known that she had woken up from her nap and now wanted someone—or everyone—to pay attention to her. Eve sighed, then flashed an apologetic smile at her guests. Dessert was going to have to wait. "Looks like I'm being paged."

"Why don't you do what you need to do?" Josiah suggested gently. "I can entertain your little bundle of joy for a few minutes. If I'm not mistaken, I haven't had the pleasing experience of holding the young lady yet," he added.

Bless Josiah, she thought. "All right, then, she's all yours." She turned to look at Adam. "Adam, could you please—"

She didn't have to finish her request. He knew what she needed him to do. Pushing himself away from the table, Adam rose to his feet. "No problem. I'll go get her for you."

Brooklyn had napped in the family room where the baby could easily be seen by her parents during dinner. Walking into the family room now, Adam bent over the port-a-crib and picked his daughter up.

A quick check of her diaper told him she was still miraculously dry, although he had to admit that the thought of depositing a slightly soggy infant onto Josiah's lap did have its appeal. Something about the older man didn't sit quite right. It was only a matter of time before he figured out why.

Holding his daughter, aware of her every movement and how incredibly soft she felt against him, Adam crossed back to the dining room. He made his way over to Josiah.

"Ah, there's the lovely lady. The spitting image of her mother," Josiah declared, his thin lips curving in a faint smile. He put out his arms, looking forward to holding the little girl.

Adam hesitated for a beat. "You know how to hold a baby?" he heard himself asking.

Damn, when had that happened? When had he begun making noises like some overprotective, clucking mother hen?

Josiah raised his gray eyes to look at him. The steely eyes reminded him of laser beams. "I've held a few babies in my time, Mr. Smythe," Josiah answered.

Banking down a reluctance that had no rhyme or reason to it, Adam handed his daughter over to the other man. Josiah accepted the small, wriggling bundle, a look akin to awe gracing the gaunt face.

It was Adam's turn to study the old man. There was no hesitation, no awkwardness. Josiah held the little girl as if he'd had infinite practice doing so. And then he remembered.

"Eve told me that you have a daughter."

"I do. And a granddaughter," Josiah added, never taking his eyes away from the baby in his arms.

"So I guess that makes you an old hand at this." Adam found that if he engaged someone in conversation enough times, eventually, he found what he was after.

Josiah spared him the most fleeting of glances, his attention completely focused on the tiny human being in his arms. "I wasn't around very much when my daughter was this age and by the time her daughter was, they were in England, so no, I'm not an old hand at this. Some things just require the right instincts," he pronounced.

The man became more and more of an enigma. "And what is it that *you* did for a living when you worked?" Adam asked, turning the tables on the older man.

"Whatever I had to," Josiah replied quietly, his attention still exclusively focused on the bright, animated small face before him. The barest hint of a smile graced his lips as he added, "You might say I was a jack-of-all-trades. Good at all," he added, changing the old saying to suit him. "The fact that I survived attests to my ability to remain alive even in the most adverse conditions."

He knew even less than he knew before, Adam thought. But now wasn't the time to continue digging. He had a strong suspicion that Josiah enjoyed weaving answers that went around in circles.

Adam nodded toward the kitchen. "If you're okay, I'll go lend Eve a hand."

"Of course I'm okay." Josiah addressed his answer to Brooklyn. He looked—and felt—younger just by holding this radiant life form. Powerful medicine, he mused, these newborns. "Why shouldn't I be?" he challenged mildly, finally looking up at Adam. "Go, help Eve. She isn't as strong as she'd like to believe she is. It usually takes more than a month to recover from bringing a child into the world."

Josiah said it with authority, as if familiar with the process. Just who was this old man who saw himself as Eve's benefactor and secret guardian? He hadn't a clue. Yet. But he would, he promised himself. He would.

Adam went to the kitchen, crossing paths with Lucas. The driver, finished loading the dishwasher, was on his way back to the dining room. The man nodded at him the way one tenant passing another in an apartment complex might, anonymous but friendly.

What was *his* story? Adam couldn't help wondering. Lucas looked a little too robust, too buff under his uniform to be just a driver. Did he double as the old man's bodyguard? And why would Josiah need a bodyguard?

"How much do you know about Josiah?" Adam asked Eve, lowering his voice so he wouldn't be overheard by the men in the other room.

The question surprised her. She regarded Josiah with nothing but deep affection. Being around the older man made her feel as if a piece of her father was still alive. "I've known Josiah all my life."

That didn't answer his question. He was certain that there'd been people who'd known Ted Bundy all their lives—or thought they had.

"But what do you *know* about him?" Adam pressed.

She stopped decorating the pumpkin dessert and turned to face Adam. "That he's a lonely old man who's very sweet and occasionally takes in rescued dogs when his own pass on." Her eyes narrowed as she looked at him, trying to guess what this was actually all about. "Why?"

Adam shrugged dismissively. "No reason. He's just trying to stare me down."

"He's curious about you," she corrected, going back to putting the finishing touches on one of the desserts. Shaking the can of whipped cream, she added a swirl right on the top, then drizzled the finished product with a handful of crushed pecans. "He thinks my judgment might be influenced by the fact that you are, after all, very good-looking and you're Brooklyn's father."

His mouth curved in amusement. "You really think I'm handsome?"

She pretended to be engrossed in what she was doing. "I believe the exact description I used was 'good-looking.'"

He was grinning now, not just smiling. "You want to quibble?"

What she wanted to do, Eve realized with a sudden jolt to her entire system, was make love with him. She found it unnerving that nothing had really changed. That incredible attraction that had drawn her to him in the first place was still there, alive and well. Perhaps even stronger than it had been originally.

The question was, what to do about it? Would she ignore what she was feeling, or give in to it?

Could she trust him, or was she just being an idiot? She really wished she knew, but the jury was still out on that.

Eve took a breath, trying to clear her head and focus. Finished with the whipped cream, she placed the last dessert onto the tray on the counter and then turned to Adam. "Would you carry that in for me, please?"

He paused to take in her handiwork, seeing it for the first time. He'd been too lost in thought to pay attention to what she was actually doing.

"This is like in a restaurant where they bring out a cart with a whole bunch of desserts for the customer to choose from," he observed. Josiah had brought a traditional apple pie with him. Obviously Eve had forgotten that she'd asked him to and had put in a great deal of work on this array. "When did you get a chance to do all this?"

"Yesterday afternoon while Brooklyn was napping. Cooking and creating different desserts relaxes me," she explained, though she figured he probably thought that was strange.

Making love relaxes me.

Adam stopped abruptly, slanting a look at Eve. Had he just said that out loud?

No, thank God. Judging by the expression on her face, he'd managed to keep his unexpected remark safe in the recesses of his mind. It was a lot better for both of them if it remained there.

Picking up the tray, Adam followed her back into the dining room.

Josiah's face lit up. The older man had, she knew, a sweet tooth that was never satisfied. "I'll have one of everything," he told her before Adam had a chance to set the tray down.

"I've got a feeling he's not kidding," Adam commented to Eve in a stage whisper.

Sitting beside his employer, shaking his keys above Brooklyn to entertain her, Lucas glanced in Adam's direction. "He's not," he confirmed.

"Why would I joke about something like that?" Josiah asked. "I have a weakness for pumpkin pie—pumpkin in any form," he added. His eyes swept over the offerings. He was unable to make up his mind. "It's times like this that I lament the fact that we have but one stomach instead of four, like cows."

"You can take some of them with you," Eve told him. She reached for her daughter, who was still in the crook of Josiah's arm. "Here, let me take her so that you can eat."

But Josiah shook his head, maintaining his arm around the baby. "She's fine where she is, Eve. She won't interfere," he assured her.

To prove it, he drew over the pumpkin parfait she'd made and sank his spoon into the center of the whipped cream. Bringing the spoon to his mouth, he closed his eyes for a moment and made a deep, satisfied sound as he savored the taste.

"You know, Eve," he said, his eyes still closed, "if you ever decide to stop being a veterinarian, you might consider becoming a pastry chef." He opened his eyes to see her reaction. "I'd stake you to opening up your own restaurant."

He noticed that Adam was studying him the exact same way he had studied the other man earlier. Josiah guessed at the reason. Adam was trying to figure out just where he had gotten all his money. The answer was a great deal simpler than the man would have dreamed. "The trick is to invest wisely and to know when to pull out."

"I didn't ask anything," Adam pointed out, somewhat surprised at the unsolicited advice that had just come his way.

"Not verbally," Josiah acknowledged, an enigmatic smile barely registering at the corners of his mouth. "But your eyes did."

Brooklyn shifted, waving her tiny arms. The scent of the tantalizing spices that had gone into making the dessert seemed to register. She began to fuss.

This couldn't be comfortable for Josiah, Eve thought. Again she reached to take her baby from him.

"Let me—" Eve started, but she never got the chance to complete the offer.

"You sit and take it easy," Adam told her. "I can take her."

He saw Josiah about to protest, but then decided to keep his peace. He didn't bother wondering what was up. He just took his daughter into his arms.

Chapter 11

Sitting on the sofa, Eve stretched her legs out so that they went far beneath the coffee table. She allowed her eyes to close for a moment. A long sigh escaped her lips. Josiah and Lucas had departed more than half an hour ago, leaving a host of compliments in their wake. Adam had insisted on putting Brooklyn to bed. With the table cleared and the dishes done, there was nothing left for her to do except enjoy the stillness.

Which she did, finding it almost seductive. She stretched out her legs a little farther.

"Tired?"

Her eyes flew open and she shifted in her seat, turning to look at Adam. But he had already rounded the sofa, dropping down on the cushion next to hers.

She smiled at him, infinitely grateful that he was

here, taking care of her. Who would have ever thought things would arrange themselves this way? Eight months ago, all she wanted to do was get away from him and the life she thought he represented.

"Yes," she admitted, quickly adding, "but very satisfied." She wanted this moment, this contented feeling to go on for a little longer. "It felt good doing that, hosting a dinner," she told him. "I didn't realize how much I missed cooking. Not that I don't appreciate all the take-out meals that found their way into my kitchen," she interjected quickly. Her eyes searched his face, afraid that Adam would take her initial words the wrong way.

He could almost read her mind. The idea made him laugh. "I wasn't about to take offense," he assured her. "And between you and me, your cooking tonight outstripped anything that I brought home this last month."

He realized his slip a second after it had come out of his mouth. He's referred to Eve's house as home. Not *her* home, but just "home."

Had she picked up on that? Looking at her, he couldn't tell.

He supposed in the last few weeks, he had come to think of Eve's place as home. Her house was where he spent most of his downtime.

Moreover, this was where his daughter was.

Careful, Serrano. You're just here to look after her, to make sure the scum you're associating with doesn't harm her or the baby. Nothing more. Don't let yourself get caught up in something you can't handle.

The father of her child. Eve realized she was smiling at him. Maybe it was the afterglow of a successful dinner party, small though it was. Or maybe she was just too tired to keep her guard up, but she was having some very kind, not to mention sensual, thoughts about Adam right now.

Maybe she'd been too hard on him.

After all, he didn't have to come around all these weeks and help her until she finally got her "mother" legs firmly planted beneath her. But Adam had come through for her with flying colors.

All this after she had, in essence, run out on him.

Don't forget why you ran out on him.

But he'd changed, Eve silently argued with herself.

She'd tried to cling to the belief that people were basically good and that, if they went down the wrong path, with enough effort, they could redeem themselves. They could get back to the right path again. There was nothing to indicate Adam had brought his old way of life with him or that he was still associating with addicts.

When would he have the time? His days were divided between the bookstore and the baby and her.

"You're awfully quiet," Adam observed after several minutes of silence had gone by. Despite her arguing to the contrary, *had* all this been too much for her? She usually wasn't this quiet. "What are you thinking?"

Not wanting to admit that she'd been thinking about him, that lately, most of her thoughts were centered on or around him, Eve said, "I was just thinking about going back to work at the animal hospital on Monday. Vera has been pretty swamped and she's had to close the place on Sundays. I don't like not being available to my patients one day a week."

He knew her. If she went back, she'd throw herself into her work wholeheartedly. It was easier to watch over her in her house. A lot of people came into the hospital. An assailant could easily slip in.

"You think you're up to going back full-time?" he asked. "Maybe you should try going back just part-time for now, work your way back up to frantic over the course of a month or two."

She'd already made up her mind. There was a place for the baby in the back office. She, Vera and Susannah could all take turns keeping an eye on Brooklyn.

"I don't like just dipping my toe in the water," she told him. "I like diving in."

The smile that came to his lips was automatic. "Yes, I remember."

Her cheeks suddenly turned a fascinating shade of scarlet. Adam did his best to bite back a laugh. As he did, he felt that same strong, breath-stealing stir whirl around his insides, the one he experienced whenever he would look at her, *really* look at her and realize just how beautiful she was.

Allowing his instincts to govern him, the way he would during a mission, Adam brushed his knuckles against her cheek. He saw a glimmer of desire flash in her eyes. Considering what was at stake, that should have been his red flag, his signal to back away. Now.

But he ignored it.

Ignored everything but this unmanageable yearning that was holding him a veritable prisoner. With one hand gently touching her face, Adam leaned in and lightly brushed his lips against hers.

Though his lips barely touched hers, it still had the

same effect as the first time he'd kissed her all those months ago. He felt as if a fist had been slammed into his midsection, knocking all the air right out of him.

Okay, this was where he *had to* pull back. He'd had his sample, had tasted how sweet her lips still were and had rediscovered just how overwhelmingly susceptible he still was to her. All his questions were concisely answered.

This was where he needed to cut and run, or at the very least, to retreat. There was no way this could lead to anything except for frustration. And the more he allowed this longing, this need, to build up within him, the more frustrated he'd be. There was no recourse but to leave. The woman had just given birth, for God's sake. She was literally in no shape to give him what he so badly craved—and that was a good thing because, deep in his soul, he knew she was a habit he needed to kick.

For her sake.

He had nothing to offer her except for bits and pieces of himself and a life that was forever being lived on the edge. If she were part of his world, *really* a part of his world, she'd be in danger all the time. And he would be worried about her all the time, her *and* the baby. The first thing he'd been taught was that an operative with a split focus was a dead operative.

He couldn't let himself go, for her sake more than for his.

So, with supreme effort, Adam drew away, his adrenaline racing through his veins as if he had his back to the wall and was facing down an entire squadron of drug dealers, every last one of them intent on slowly vivisecting him.

Stunned, Eve blinked. Oh, no, he wasn't going to do this to her. He wasn't going to stir her up, making her, in the space of hardly a few seconds, mentally forsake each and every one of the promises she'd made to herself just to pull back.

Was he trying to prove something to himself? That he could walk away from her at any time? Or was there more to it? Was he showing her that he still had power over her? That he could still press her buttons, make her need him more than she needed the very air to breathe?

Well, she would be doing the showing, not him.

Very deliberately, Eve wove her arms around his neck, her eyes more than her arms holding him in place. The next moment, she brought her mouth to his. Brought her soul to his, kissing him as if the very world would be doomed if she didn't.

Damn it, Eve, why are you making this so hard?

Pulling his head back, Adam gently but firmly removed her arms from around his neck. "We can't," was all he said.

She put her own interpretation to his words, praying she wasn't being the biggest fool the world had ever seen. That he wasn't just toying with her because he could.

"I'm all right," she whispered, her eyes on his. "The doctor told me that I could…be with you if I wanted to."

Be with you. What a tenderly innocent way to say it, he couldn't help thinking. Maybe, just maybe, if he could just have this one last time to make love with her, that would somehow sustain him. He knew all too well that making love with her wouldn't quench the fire, but at least it could dowse it for a small space of time, allowing him to reapply himself to what he really needed to concentrate on. With any luck, the worthless piece of trash he was dealing with would slip, giving him the name of the head supplier and the department could move in for the kill.

He wasn't naive enough to think that once this present head of the cartel was captured that would be the end of it. Like a hydra monster, if one head was cut off, one if not two more would suddenly pop up in its place. But with luck, there would be some downtime and maybe, the department could further clean up the streets.

With effort, they might make it more difficult for a new foothold to form in the high schools currently being supplied with narcotics. Any respite was better than none and who knew, maybe in that small time frame the users would see the upside of even partially regaining control over their lives. Maybe they would think twice before abdicating it again, allowing powders, pills and drug dealers to govern them.

But right at this moment, Adam had to admit that he had a great deal of sympathy for addicts. For the first time in his life, he could see things from their perspective because he was addicted to Eve. Addicted to the rush she created in his veins. Addicted to the memory of what was and to the incredible draw of the promise of what could be.

He *needed* her and could think of absolutely nothing else.

Was she losing the battle? Or was Adam trying to be strong for reasons she couldn't grasp? Eve didn't know.

All she knew was that she needed him. Badly. It was as if their lovemaking had taken place in another life, a life she needed to get back to.

She raised her eyes to his, silently entreating him. And then, when he made no move to take her back into his arms, she finally put it into words, quietly saying, "Adam, don't make me beg."

Her voice was low, but the need she felt pulsated throughout her entire being.

"No begging," he promised, his own voice husky with longing.

The next moment, Adam covered her mouth with his own, kissing her deeply. In less than a heartbeat, he became lost within her.

Sealed by that physical act alone, they were instantly one. Nothing mattered right now to Adam but this over-whelming, screaming need inside of him, this need that demanded satisfaction, some sort of an outlet before it completely tore him apart.

The moment he silently surrendered control, it was as if someone had suddenly fired a starter pistol in the air, signaling the beginning of this explosive interlude. Adam found himself hardly able to remember how he got from one stage to another. Couldn't actually recall how his clothes had disappeared from his body. One second, he was dressed, the next, he wasn't. Had he done it, or had she? He was unclear as to the steps. Similarly, he wasn't even sure if his hands had urgently tugged her dress from her while she had been similarly engaged with his clothes, or if they simply divested themselves of their own clothes.

He was only aware of movement and shedding.

Through it all, his mouth remained urgently sealed to hers as if his very life depended on it.

In a way, it did.

And just like that, she was nude. Her flesh was tender and pliant beneath his hands. He felt as if he was on fire just touching her, sliding his palms along her soft, soft breasts, caressing her supple curves and re-committing them to memory.

This was only the second time he'd made love with her, and yet every touch, every pass, teased forth a memory from within him. Her body was oh-so-familiar to him even though, as he trailed his hands along her curves, he felt on the brink of an exciting new adventure.

Over and over again his mouth slanted over hers, kissing the sensitive area along her throat, seeking out the hollow of her neck, the dip in her now-flat belly. Her moan of pleasure in response to his questing tongue set him off the way Adam thought nothing ever could, making his head spin.

She had never told Adam that he was her first lover. It wasn't the kind of thing a woman broadcasted, even though, in her case, she had never met anyone she'd wanted in her bed. In her heart, however, Eve was certain that someone with Adam's experience would know. She, on the other hand, had nothing to compare except perhaps the first time that he'd been with her. What she vividly recalled was that she'd been utterly, hopelessly lost in ecstasy.

This time around, the ecstasy had doubled itself so that she could hardly contain the wild feelings rushing through her. It was as close to an out-of-body experience as she would ever hope to have.

She didn't want it to end.

Something told her this would only be a onetime thing. Last time, there'd been no encores because she'd discovered his secret life. This time around, she had a feeling that the cause for the lack of encores would be his.

But if it came to that, she wanted this isolated moment in time to last as long as possible.

Eve bit down on her lower lip as the first climax suddenly exploded over her, a depth charge coming from oblivion and targeting her. There'd been almost no warning. One moment, there was deliciously mounting pleasure, the next moment, fireworks.

Bucking, raising her hips to absorb every ray of heat, every movement of his mouth over her inner core, she cried out his name and something more. With lightning flashing through her brain, Eve couldn't even say for certain what it was that she had cried out.

But Adam could.

He'd heard it even though he told himself he'd imagined it.

At moments like this, with control wrenched away from him, it was easy to hear things that weren't said, see things that weren't there.

With his last scrap of strength, he forced himself to deny what part of him had thought he'd heard, burying the words "I love you," even though, with all his heart, he wished he could acknowledge them, press them to his chest and echo them in kind.

Instead, he drew himself up along her body, igniting them both as flesh rubbed against flesh. And just like that, he was hovering over her, looking down into her eyes, his gut tightening. Feeling things he couldn't acknowledge, wanting to say things he couldn't say.

It was just the moment that caused him to get carried away, nothing more, Adam silently swore to himself.

Even so, he gathered her into his arms, holding himself back as much as he could while positioning his hips over hers.

And then he was inside again, entering as gently as he could, ever alert for any sign that he was hurting her. That she had, at the last moment, changed her mind.

There was no sign.

Her arms tightened around his neck and she held on as hard as she could, mimicking the rhythm of his hips, determined to feel the peak of the crescendo at the same moment as he did. And then, it seized her, sending a rainbow of stars shooting all through her. She held on as hard as she could, praying that the moment would never end.

Mourning because she knew it had to.

Chapter 12

At first, Eve couldn't register the sound on the outer perimeter of her consciousness. Still in the throes of the final stages of euphoria, it took her several seconds to identify the insistent, soft buzzing.

A cell phone, set on vibrate.

Since hers played the first few bars of "When the Saints Go Marching In," a song she vividly remembered from her childhood, Eve knew the buzzing cell phone had to belong to Adam.

The last vapors of her euphoric state evaporated. The outside world invaded this piece of paradise they'd managed to construct. It was to be expected.

But on Thanksgiving?

Because she'd unwittingly stumbled across Adam's double life eight months ago, unbidden suspicions instantly crowded her brain. She tried to fight her doubts. Harboring suspicions would taint this perfect moment for her.

They already did.

The cell phone stopped and then started ringing again. And again. Whoever was on the other end obviously didn't want to go to voice mail. Eve suppressed a sigh.

"Your phone's buzzing," she finally said.

He was aware of that. He'd secretly been hoping that his caller would go away. But no such luck.

It was either his handler, or the reason he was being handled.

The phone vibrated again.

"Shouldn't you answer it?" Eve asked, wondering why he wasn't. Fearing that she knew.

Adam turned to look at her. All he wanted to do at this moment was make love with her again.

"I don't want to," he told her truthfully.

Was that because he couldn't take the call with her so close, or because Adam was having the same thoughts about the moment as she was? That it was too perfect to spoil.

Too late.

Shifting, she moved away from him and began patting the articles of clothing entangled and scattered all over the floor, searching for the telltale lump that was his phone. Adam instantly came to life and started looking for the offending cell phone himself. He needed to get to it before she did.

But Eve found his cell phone first. Pulling it out of the pocket of his jeans, she glanced at the LCD screen as she held the phone up to him. "You'd better answer it. They don't sound like they're going to go away."

He glanced down at the display. It said "Private." That would be his handler.

Flipping the phone open, Adam murmured, "Hello?" as his mind scrambled, searching for a way to get rid of the man without arousing Eve's suspicions.

"Where the hell were you? I called your damn phone four separate times."

"Three," Adam corrected, keeping his voice even. "And it's Thanksgiving."

"Yeah, I know. My wife's not happy about me ducking out on her and her family. The whole bunch should be locked up in an insane asylum," he grumbled, allowing himself a personal moment.

It wasn't like Hugh to complain about his life. His handler was careful to keep a definite line drawn between his work and his private world. Adam couldn't help wondering if something within the mission was going south. "What's so important it can't wait until tomorrow?"

Hugh's tone was clip. "Intel has it that the incoming shipment's been moved up. Might not be accurate, but get ready to roll in the next couple of days or so anyway. Might even be tonight," he amended. "Whoever that college punk's main man is, he keeps everyone on their toes."

Adam focused on the only thing he considered crucial. "Tonight?" He saw Eve looking at him, the curiosity in her eyes growing.

"Maybe," Hugh responded. "I just wanted you to be on standby."

"Right," Adam muttered.

The connection on the other end of the line went dead.

Glancing toward Eve, Adam continued talking as if his caller was still there. "Well, you handle it. I've got faith in you. Call the police and give them whatever information you can pull from the surveillance tapes. Okay, fine. If they want to talk to me, I can come down to the store to answer questions. But try to handle it yourself first. Yeah, Happy Thanksgiving to you, too," he added for good measure. "Goodbye."

"Police?" Eve echoed once he shut the cell phone. "What was all that about?"

Adam tossed the phone back down in the general vicinity of his jeans. He sighed and shook his head, as if the idea of vandalism was beyond him. "That was the new clerk I hired last week. He said the security company called him because someone tripped the alarm, breaking into the bookstore tonight. Can you believe it? On Thanksgiving. Whoever it was that broke in probably figured nobody would be around."

She pulled her dress up to her chest, partially covering herself. It seemed strange somehow to be carrying on a conversation naked like this, with the heat of passion drifting into the horizon.

"This security system you have, it's hooked up to a surveillance camera, right?" she asked.

He found her sliver of modesty really arousing.

"Absolutely," he told her. "I've got a lot of valuable books in that shop. And some of them are rare, one-of-a-kind editions. Doesn't make any sense not to have an interactive security system."

She thought of the pure joy she'd seen on her father's face when she'd given him that Mark Twain first edition for his birthday. "I'm sorry," she said with feeling. "What did they take?"

She was being so sympathetic, he felt guilty about lying to her. "Bill has to go over the inventory to see what's missing."

"But he's sure someone broke in...?"

Adam nodded. "He said the security company said that the alarm was tripped."

"Could just be a faulty system," she suggested hopefully. "Maybe nothing was taken."

"That's always a possibility," he agreed. He'd forgotten how optimistic she could be. It was one of the things about her that reached out to him.

She shook her head, crossing her arms before her tightly. "Books should be sacred."

"Nothing is sacred," Adam responded, looking at her intently. *Except, maybe for you.*

"Do you think you should go, make a report?" she suggested, mentally crossing her fingers that he wouldn't feel the need to do so.

"No, Bill can handle it. He spent the holiday with friends and was on his way home when the security company called him—"

"Why him and not you?" she asked.

"Because I knew I wouldn't want to be interrupted," he told her, his eyes caressing her. "Bill has no family here so he can handle it for the time being, unless the police need to talk to me," he said.

Banishing Hugh's call from his mind, as well as the fact that he'd been forced to lie to her again, Adam gave in to his urges. He gathered Eve into his arms. The heat of her body stirred him just as much now as it had before they'd come together tonight.

He swept the hair away from her face. "Now, where were we?"

He watched the smile bloom on her face. "In ecstasy as I remember," she teased.

"Ecstasy, right. Sounds familiar," he agreed, bringing his mouth down to hers.

There were no more calls that night. He'd made sure that he'd shut off his cell phone, just this once.

Adam frowned. He could feel the tension building in his body.

Every hour that passed without a call from the cocky Scderholm was another hour in which to wonder if something within the operation had gone desperately awry. Or if whoever currently headed up this deadly daisy chain was on to him and had decided to pull up stakes, cutting his losses before the trap snapped around him.

There was no way of telling. Hugh's informants on the street, as well as the one that he himself had cultivated, said there were no rumors about a possible shift in power or even that a shipment was being moved.

It was as if no one knew anything, a highly unlikely scenario.

Adam grew progressively antsy, but at least he had a story in place if he had to suddenly leave Eve's house.

Unless, of course, the play went down in the wee hours of the night, he thought darkly, nodding his head at his last customer of the day as he rang up a rather worn copy of *The Catcher in the Rye.*

Walking the man to the door, Adam flipped over the closed sign and secured the locks.

Ten minutes later, he was on the road, his thoughts reverting back to the precarious situation he was in. Again.

Although the narcissistic college kid had a flare for the dramatic, Adam was fairly certain that he didn't have to worry about a middle-of-the-night call from the supplier. He knew for a fact that Sederholm preferred conducting his business in the light of day. Despite his bravado and incredibly poor imitation of Al Pacino, the brash student felt safer when he didn't have to remain alert, worrying about who or what was hiding in the shadows.

Practically on automatic pilot, Adam blinked and realized he needed to turn off on a street where a strip mall was still in its infancy. He'd decided to pay Eve a surprise visit. This was where Eve and Vera had moved their practice in order to accommodate the needs of their growing clientele. The new animal hospital had space for new X-ray machines.

This was the best part of his day, Adam thought. The part where he got to see Eve and the baby. Where he got to pretend that he was actually just a regular person with a regular life.

For how much longer?

He shut away the annoying voice in his head.

Because of what he did, there was no point in his thinking too far ahead. All he had was right now and he intended to make the most of it, the most of every moment he had with his family.

His family. It had a nice ring. Even if it was a false one.

As he pulled into the parking lot situated before the Laguna Animal Hospital, Adam didn't see her car. Eve usually parked off to the side, leaving the area right before the hospital entrance clear for her four-legged patients and their owners. Right now, the parking lot was fairly empty. Where was Eve's car?

Something was wrong. He could feel it.

Susannah was seated behind the front desk, focused on several beige folders spread out before her. She was working on their billing statements. The brunette looked up the moment she heard the door open. Recognizing him, the perfunctory smile she flashed at the owners of their patients faded. In its place was a look of grave concern.

He was right. Something was wrong. Ever mindful of his surroundings and the dangerous tightrope he walked, Adam swept his eyes over the immediate area. But nothing seemed out of place.

"Hello, Mr. Smythe."

There was a note of hesitation in her voice. Was the animal technician debating telling him something? Again Adam glanced around, searching for some tell-tale sign that would give him a clue. Had one of Sederholm's lowlifes come here to threaten Eve?

He dispensed with the niceties. "Where's Dr. Walters, Susannah?" he asked the technician.

Susannah seemed genuinely distressed as she began her narrative. "Dr. Walters had to rush to the hospital."

His brain instantly spun scenarios. He forced himself to bank them down. Eve was a veterinarian. Susannah could be referring to the emergency animal trauma center located in Bedford.

"Why did she have to rush off, Susannah?" he asked, striving for patience.

"It's the baby," the receptionist blurted out.

Okay, now he could panic. "What about the baby?"

One word came tumbling out after another. "Brooklyn started coughing and sneezing and it looked like she was really having trouble breathing. Dr. Walters called Brooklyn's pediatrician—"

"Name, I need a name," he said, interrupting her when he couldn't recall the physician's name.

All he could remember was that it was a woman and that she was associated with the same hospital, Blair Memorial, that the ambulance had taken her to right after Eve had given birth to their daughter.

Susannah stopped dead for a moment, apparently drawing a blank.

"It's Dr. Collins," Vera told him, walking into the reception area from the rear of the clinic. Eve's associate heard Adam's voice and came out to fill him in. "Dr. Sarah Collins," she specified. "Dr. Collins told Eve to meet her with the baby in Blair Memorial's E.R." Approaching the desk, the short, ordinarily perky blonde pulled out a pad and a pen from her lab coat pocket. "I can give you the address—"

"No need," he thanked her, hurrying out again. "I've already got it."

"I offered to drive her," Vera called out after him, following him to the door. "But she wanted someone to stay to take care of the dogs scheduled for appointments."

That sounded like Eve all right. Even in the middle of a possible crisis, her mind was on her responsibilities. Hell of a woman, he thought.

"Don't worry," Vera yelled after him, holding the door open so he could hear her. "Brooklyn's going to be just fine."

"Thanks," was all he managed to shout back.

The next moment, he was in his car, slamming the door. His heart raced as he gunned the engine. He'd been in life-and-death situations where a single word could blow his cover and hadn't felt half as apprehensive as he did right at this moment.

Being a father changed you. He'd never fully appreciated that until this very minute.

Traffic was heavy this time of day. Not wanting to get hemmed in by gridlock, he avoided the freeway altogether and took side streets instead. With one eye on his rearview mirror, ever on the lookout for police cars that might further impede his progress, Adam drove to the hospital as if his engine was on fire and he needed to reach his destination before it exploded.

For the first time since his sister had overdosed, he prayed.

The nurse at the information desk looked as if she was ready to summon one of the security guards. With effort, Adam lowered his voice and reined in both his impatience and his fear. "Look, my little girl was brought in a little while ago. She's only six weeks old. Dr. Sarah Collins is her doctor—"

At the mention of the doctor's name, the nurse seemed mollified. "Why didn't you say so?" Typing something into the computer database, she skimmed her finger along the resulting list that appeared on the monitor. "What's your daughter's name?"

"Brooklyn. Brooklyn Walters." He was going to get that changed as soon as he could, he thought. He wanted there to be no doubt that she was his.

"They admitted her. Second floor. Room 213." She raised her eyes to his face. "The elevators are—"

But he was already running not toward the elevators, but to the stairwell. He could make faster time on his own instead of waiting for the elevator.

Brooklyn had been admitted. This was worse than he thought.

Adam stopped short in the doorway of 213. There were five cribs inside the room. Four of them were empty. The one in the middle was not. Encased in a see-through plastic tent, the sight of which made his blood run cold, Adam saw his daughter.

She looked tiny. Tinier somehow than she had when she was born. And he had never felt so utterly helpless in his life.

It took him a second to take the rest of the room in and realize that Eve was sitting in the chair beside the crib. Keeping vigil.

Crossing the threshold, he came up behind her. With his hands on either side of her shoulders, he bent over and kissed the top of her head.

Eve never took her eyes off the face of the sleeping infant in the oxygen tent. Reaching up for the hand on her right shoulder, she laced her fingers through his, silently taking comfort from the contact.

She'd sensed Adam's presence the moment he'd entered the room. All afternoon, when she wasn't praying for the baby's recovery, she'd been praying that he would come. All her attempts to reach him on his cell had ended with irritating messages conveyed to her by a metallic voice. Signals were not going through.

Eve liked to think of herself as a strong person. She believed that she was able to handle anything that came her way. She had so far. But the mere possibility of something happening to her daughter had completely undone her.

There was a lump in her throat and she had trouble talking through it, even after clearing her throat twice. "Dr. Collins says she's going to be all right," she whispered. Her voice cracked as she felt tears choking her.

"I know. I ran into her in the hall." He'd rushed to the baby's room when he all but ran right into the woman. She'd given him a brief update, starting with the prognosis and working her way backward. He came around to stand beside Eve, next to the crib. "Why didn't you call me? I would have dropped everything."

"I did. But I couldn't get through and I didn't want to leave her to go looking for a pay phone." She pressed her lips together, gazing at Brooklyn. The baby had been so uncomfortable earlier. "She looks so little and helpless in there."

Adam shook his head. "She might be little, but she's not helpless. She's like her mother, a fighter," he told her. In his heart, he held on to that. On to the good news that Dr. Collins had given him. That Brooklyn was responding to the medication. Right now, he was concerned about Eve. "Have you had anything to eat?"

"I don't know," she answered truthfully. Turning from the crib, she looked up at him. "I don't think so. It all happened so suddenly. First a sniffle, then a tiny cough—it almost sounded cute." She should have been paying closer attention, she silently upbraided herself. "And then she was having trouble breathing." Eve paused to take a deep breath, trying to still her rapid pulse. "I was never so scared in my life."

"But she's okay," he reminded Eve, his voice, low, soothing. "Dr. Collins said Brooklyn was just staying here overnight to make sure everything was all right. Lots of kids get the croup."

She didn't care about lots of kids, all she cared about was *this* kid. "But she's not even two months old."

"All her vitals are fine." Taking her hand, he raised Eve to her feet. "She's going to be fine. And look at the bright side."

"Bright side?" Eve echoed, puzzled.

He brushed her hair out of her eyes and smiled at her. "Yes. You can hold this over her head when she acts out."

With a laugh that was half a cry, Eve turned to him and buried her head in his chest, grateful beyond words that he was here with her.

And then all the self-control she'd employed, holding tightly on to her panic, her fears, dissolved. Her fingers wrapped in his shirt, Eve felt the dam break inside of her. There was no holding back the tears.

Chapter 13

"You're sure about this?" Josiah inquired, his tone giving no clue that the information surprised him.

The deep, slightly raspy voice on the other end of the landline answered, "Absolutely."

Just for a moment, Josiah closed his eyes, absorbing what he'd just been told. Who would have thought? And then he took a breath and said, "Thanks, Harry. I owe you one."

The man known as "Harry" to only an assorted few chuckled. "You owe me five, Turner, but who's counting?"

"You, obviously. And you still have trouble with your sums." Moving forward on the finely creased brown leather chair that had memorized his imprint from years of use, Josiah prepared to hang up. "See you on Saturday as usual?"

"Wouldn't miss it."

The receiver made contact with its cradle. Sitting back again, Josiah stared off into space, reviewing what he had just learned.

The truth was a lot better than he'd thought. It removed the need of having to do away with Eve's Adam. He hadn't been in a position to have to rely on that set of skills in a while. Admittedly, he'd gotten a little rusty although he knew that ultimately it was like riding a bike. You never really forget. Still, his eyesight wasn't what it used to be. The task would have fallen to Lucas.

Josiah allowed himself a hint of a smile. His lips were not given to curving and the action was somewhat unfamiliar to them. Anyone passing by would have thought he was grimacing.

"Bad news?" Lucas asked, walking into the study less than a heartbeat after the phone conversation was terminated.

Josiah raised his eyes to look at Lucas's face. The grimace widened.

Away from prying eyes, the rapport between the two men was a great deal less formal than when they were out in public. But even so, it was a given for Lucas that Josiah was and always would be his superior, his mentor, the way it had once been when they had worked at the Bureau together. Furthermore, Lucas never lost sight of the fact that it had been Josiah who had saved his life in the field.

Unable to give a hundred percent to the job, Lucas had handed in his resignation rather than be relegated to a desk job. His life seemed to have lost its purpose.

When Josiah retired from the Bureau several months

later, he made it a point to look Lucas up and promptly hired the still young man to be his "man Friday," a position which entailed doing everything and anything that needed doing. If that included occasionally falling back on past talents and conducting a little investigating, so be it.

However, this time around, because it was Eve, Josiah had decided to undertake the investigation himself. He wound up pleasantly surprised for his trouble.

Josiah paused for a long moment before answering. "Strange news."

They had been together a long time. Lucas knew enough to wait for the older man to elaborate. Prodding Josiah usually had the opposite desired effect. The former senior special agent had the ability to imitate the tight jaws of a clam when he wanted to.

Josiah decided to share his intel with Lucas, a man who he had allowed, over the years, to get closer to him than anyone else, even his daughter. And, during that time, he had come to regard Lucas as the son he had never had, although he never said as much out loud. Words to that effect were not necessary. Besides, he had a feeling that Lucas knew anyway.

"Do you remember how upset Eve was when she first came back to Laguna?"

Lucas nodded. "She tried to hide it, but yes, I remember."

"It had to do with that bookstore owner."

"Brooklyn's father," Lucas said to clarify things.

Josiah inclined his head in agreement. "Yes. She had just begun to come around, to be her old self, and then her father died. That sent her into a tailspin. I thought she was just having trouble coping with her grief…" His voice trailed off for a moment as he relived the episode in his mind. "When she began to show, I realized she was trying to come to terms with something more than just grief." He looked directly into Lucas's eyes. "I sensed that she needed to talk to someone."

Lucas merely nodded, not saying a word. They both knew that in his day, Josiah was known to be at the top of his game when it came to getting confessions out of people. He never had to resort to torture or the threat of using it. There was just something about the way he looked at a person, about the way he made them feel—as if whatever was said behind closed doors would be understood and kept confidential even though no promises were made.

"She told me that she'd left Santa Barbara abruptly when she discovered that the man she was in love with turned out to be a drug dealer." Josiah took a breath, as if he was attempting to keep his anger under control. Lucas couldn't remember a time when he had seen the older man lose his temper, but wrath, when it came, would enter his eyes and was a terrible thing to behold. "I wasn't exactly happy to see him turn up here. I don't make it a habit of butting into other people's lives—"

"No, sir, you don't," Lucas agreed, silently congratulating himself for not giving in to a sudden, nearly overwhelming desire to laugh. The older man might have felt that he didn't interfere and although not intrusive in an obvious way, Josiah took it upon himself to handle things offstage as it were.

"Eve told me that Adam had changed. That he had come here, not looking for her, but wanting to make a fresh start. I found that highly suspicious," he went on, "for him to just 'pick' the same area that she had come to, but I didn't say anything to her. However, I could tell that Eve was concerned that his promise to her was written on the wind."

They'd been together, operatives and civilians, for close to two decades. In that time, Lucas had made a study of his former mentor and he could tell now that Josiah wanted some indication that he was interested in this unfolding tale.

Taking his cue, Lucas dutifully asked, "And was it valid?"

At this point, Josiah surprised him with a sound that passed for a laugh. "You have no idea."

Perhaps not an exact idea, Lucas thought, but from the gleam that had entered the older man's eye, he had a general notion where this story was ultimately heading.

"Adam Smythe isn't a bookstore owner, is he?"

Josiah stroked his chin and the neatly trimmed Van Dyke he sported. "No, he most certainly is not."

Lucas ventured a step further. "And he's not a drug dealer, either, is he?"

Josiah shook his head. "You do take some of the fun out of this, Lucas."

Lucas inclined his head in a silent tribute. "I was trained by a master."

Josiah's lips twitched just a little, a testament to his amusement.

"All right, *Grasshopper,*" he said, invoking the nickname of a character in a classic series that had once been a cult favorite, "you tell me. Just what is Eve's Adam?"

It wasn't hard to connect the dots once certain assumptions were made. "My guess is that he's some kind of law enforcement operative." Lucas paused, thinking. "Since drugs are involved, best bet is that he's with the DEA."

Admiration flared in Josiah's intense gray eyes. "The Bureau lost a valuable man when you decided to leave them."

Lucas shrugged away the compliment. "Since I couldn't give a hundred and ten percent anymore, it just seemed like the logical thing to do. How about you?" he asked. "What are you going to do with this information?" He had to admit that his curiosity had been aroused. "Are you going to keep it to yourself, or tell her?"

Ordinarily, other people's secrets were their own. But this wasn't exactly an ordinary set of circumstances. They involved someone he cared about. Someone he had been watching over since her unexpected return. His path was clear.

"The poor girl is worried that her baby's father might get sucked back into 'the life,'" he reminded Lucas. "The very least I can do is give Eve some peace of mind."

Lucas knew better than to even vaguely suggest that Josiah hold off in case something the DEA agent was involved in was going down. As a civilian, Josiah's allegiance was still to his country in general, but the circle of people who meant something to him was very small and he put them first whenever he could.

This was one of those times.

* * *

What a difference an hour made.

An hour ago, Eve thought ruefully, she'd been watching the clock, eager to close the clinic's doors and get home so that she could have a romantic evening with Adam.

She had everything planned: the menu, the music, even some of the conversation. And she had made it a point to stop by the mall during her lunch hour and had picked up possibly the hottest, sexiest lingerie she had ever seen.

But all her plans had come crashing down about her head when she'd stopped to leave Brooklyn with Josiah, who, along with Lucas, had agreed to babysit her daughter for the night. He'd told her more than once that he would be happy to do it. She knew he loved nothing more than playing the doting grandfather, but since his son-in-law had taken a post in England and taken the family with him, Josiah very rarely got the chance. He didn't talk about it, but she knew he missed his daughter and granddaughter a great deal.

"I'm not a sentimental man, Eve, but there are times that I do miss interacting with a child," was the way he'd put it. "Anytime you need an evening to yourself, I would be happy to look after Brooklyn."

So, when she'd had this idea of an evening of sizzling romance in the middle of what was judged by many to be the most hectic season of the year, his offer seemed perfect.

How was she to know that everything would come apart so quickly?

After patiently listening to her review Brooklyn's

routine, he'd taken the baby from her and then said, "Eve, I think you need to know something."

She had no idea why she'd felt an unsettling tightening within her stomach at his words. Still, despite the premonition, she definitely hadn't been prepared for what came next.

"What is it?" she'd asked him, her thoughts still racing around, checking off things she had listed only in her head.

Brooklyn began to fuss. He patted the baby on the back, rocking slightly as he stood before Eve. Brooklyn's fussing ceased almost instantly.

"I looked into a few things and I can assure you that you can stop worrying that Adam is going to revert back to drug dealing," he told her.

"Oh?" Her heart lodged itself in her throat. Adrenaline, masquerading as fear, filled her veins. "How can you make that kind of a claim? What have you heard?" she asked, curbing the urge at the last minute to ask, "What have you done?" instead.

To get into his narrative, Josiah backed up a little. "He was never a drug dealer to begin with," he told her, stunning her. "And his last name isn't Smythe. It's Serrano." He saw the uncertainty in her eyes and repeated the full name. "Adam Serrano."

Her head began to hurt. Where had he gathered all this information? He was a retired businessman. How did a retired businessman get this kind of information?

"How did you...?"

Josiah lifted his slight shoulders in a vague movement, then let them drop again. "I have friends who have friends."

Eve ran her fingertips over her forehead. The headache dancing just above her eyes was now imitating the sound of angry war drums. The throbbing made it difficult for her to absorb what Josiah was telling her.

With effort, she asked, "And what did these friends tell you?"

"That your Adam Smythe—Adam Serrano—is a DEA agent. It's not my practice to meddle," he added as a coda, "and I wouldn't have told you, except that I know how worried you've been that something might come up that would make Adam return to the unsavory life of a dealer. Now you know that he won't." He shifted Brooklyn slightly, moving her to his other shoulder. "You mean a great deal to me, Eve, and like it or not, with your father gone I feel a certain responsibility for your well-being. I'm sorry if I overstepped my place, but I just wanted to be sure that you weren't getting involved with someone who could really hurt you."

But I am. I did.

Eve could feel her heart breaking in half even as she struggled to smile at the older man. He meant well, but she would have really rather not have found this out now. Maybe later, definitely before, but not now when she had just managed to surmount her trust issues and gotten to a place where she felt she might just be able to move forward.

Still, none of this was Josiah's fault. "Thank you. I appreciate you looking out for me."

Gazing into her troubled eyes, Josiah couldn't help wondering if perhaps, despite her thanks, he had overstepped his ground and triggered something he should have left dormant. He wasn't sorry he'd looked into the matter, but he now regretted telling her he had.

With that in mind, he tried to do a little damage control. "The life of a law enforcement agent, especially when undercover, is not—"

She didn't want him to continue, or to make any excuses for Adam whatever-his-name-was. The information that Josiah had already given her made her feel numb all over.

"I understand."

Nothing had changed—and everything had changed. All she wanted to do was run, to bury herself somewhere. But there wasn't just her to consider anymore. She was a mother. She had responsibilities. Brooklyn came first, above everything else.

Eve pressed her lips together. "Look, if now isn't a good time—" She began to reach for the baby.

Josiah continued to hold the sleeping child against him. "Now is an excellent time," he told her. "Don't worry. I'm really quite good at this. I'll look after Brooklyn as if she were my own granddaughter."

There was no way she wanted to be alone with Adam now, much less spend a romantic evening with him. Betrayal wasn't an aphrodisiac.

"But—"

Josiah shook his head. "Not another word. You deserve a little time to yourself," he insisted. "Brooklyn will be here any time you want to come by to pick her up."

And with that, the former Special Agent closed the door.

Eve heard Josiah talking to the baby as if she were another adult. At any other time, it would have made her smile. But right now, she felt as if her very insides had been gutted.

With her heart feeling like a lead brick inside her chest, Eve turned away from house and went down the driveway to her car.

To drive to a place that no longer felt like home.

Adam had had an uneasy feeling weaving through him all day, and it was just getting bigger by the hour.

It had begun with a phone call. Danny Sederholm had seemed uncharacteristically jumpy when he called to talk to him. The usual irritating, cocky bravado the student displayed was absent. Sederholm had accidentally slipped and mentioned the head of the organization's name, Cesar Montoya, when he'd blurted out that the man was seeking another connection. It wasn't difficult for Adam to put two and two together and realize that the student was now viewing him as a threat.

It hadn't been easy, but he finally managed to convince Sederholm that he wasn't out to usurp him. That he was happy with the way things were and all he wanted was to be connected to a steady supply of cocaine, heroin and meth so that he could get back to his dealers.

Sederholm had sounded somewhat reassured when he hung up, but Adam knew that the college student could be easily swayed. If the next person Sederholm spoke to had a different spin on how things were going, the kid would buy into that. And then consequently, he might find himself in a heap of trouble.

This was getting old, Adam thought. He'd been pushing his luck for too long. It was definitely time to change the focus of his work. He needed a position within the department that didn't make him constantly feel as if he needed a shower.

Funny how things changed, he mused, getting into his car. His current life seemed to suit him, especially when he only had to think about himself. But it wasn't just him anymore and he didn't want it to be. He'd come to realize that he really wanted to be part of this new family unit. Wanted to come home to Eve and the baby not just for a little while, but on a regular, ongoing, permanent basis.

Eve.

Not for the first time today, he wondered what was up. She'd made a point of calling him this morning just before noon and saying that she didn't want him swinging by the clinic this afternoon. Instead, she wanted him to come to her house a little later than usual. She'd ended by saying that she had a surprise for him.

Just thinking about the conversation made him smile.

At the same time, his conscience nagged at him, the way it did more and more frequently these days. This charade couldn't go on. He needed to tell her exactly who he was. He knew it was against all company policy, but keeping her in the dark indefinitely wasn't right.

If he hoped to have a chance with her, he needed to let her know what he really did for a living. Not the undercover details, but everything that could be safely released without jeopardizing anyone else's life. He'd already made up his mind about coming clean.

His job was important, but if she wanted him to get out of law enforcement altogether he would do it. For her. He was no longer defined by his work. Something a great deal larger came into play now.

And once he made these changes, once he either left the department or at least took on another position, then maybe she would consider marrying him. Because his life, he'd come to realize, was incomplete without her and the baby.

He hadn't realized that he was just existing, not living, until he had something to compare it to. Eve made him feel alive in all the important ways that counted.

Whistling, he pulled up into her driveway. The garage was open and he saw her car parked inside. For the time being, he banked down all his other thoughts, along with that uneasy, nagging feeling at the back of his neck that told him something was wrong. He focused instead on the evening ahead.

An evening he was looking forward to spending with Eve and the baby.

Adam rang the doorbell and waited for a moment. When there was no answer, he rang again. He was about to knock when the door finally opened.

His eyes met hers and the greeting on his lips faded. The uneasy feeling that something was wrong was back. In spades.

Chapter 14

His survival instincts instantly kicked in. Especially when she didn't step back, didn't open the door any farther to let him in.

"What's wrong?" he asked tentatively.

Everything! her brain screamed.

When he stepped forward, she mechanically took a step back, thereby admitting him into the house when she hadn't really wanted to. Where did she begin? Eve silently demanded. She was so upset, so angry, that fragments of sentences crowded her mind.

One thought stood out.

Her eyes narrowed into angry, blazing slits. "You lied to me."

The accusation drove a chill down his spine. He scrambled to make sense of it. Was she talking about the past or something current? Had she found out about his dealing with Sederholm and taken it at face value, thinking he had reverted back to the life of a drug dealer?

Adam schooled himself to remain calm. Maybe this all had some sort of logical explanation he hadn't thought of yet.

"About?" he asked cautiously.

"About?" she echoed incredulously, stunned and furious at the same time. "Just exactly how many things do I have to choose from?"

So many you wouldn't believe it.

Out loud, he tried to select his words calmly, to keep from inciting her further. "I only meant that maybe there's been some mistake and that you—"

She jumped on the word. "Mistake? I'll say there's been a mistake."

Eve felt angry tears gathering in her eyes and she fisted her hands at her sides, willing them away. She wasn't about to cry in front of him. She absolutely refused to let him see how hurt she was.

"And I made it when I thought that you and I could actually put everything behind us and build something together. Have some kind of trust together. Shows what an idiot I am." Her eyes were all but shooting sparks. "Or maybe it shows how desperate I am to make our relationship work. And you, obviously, don't feel the same way." She waved her hand at the door he'd just closed behind him. "Please leave."

For a moment, he was absolutely speechless. Where had all this fury come from? "What?"

Eve ground out the words. "I said leave."

At a loss, he grasped at the first thing that came to his mind. "Is this some kind of postpartum depression you're going through?"

He couldn't have picked anything worse to say if he tried. It was akin to waving a huge red flag in front of her.

"Oh, just because I'm a woman, right away my feelings have to be pinned on a hormonal imbalance? Well, my hormones are fine, thank you very much. They're not the ones that betrayed me." Since he wouldn't do the right thing and go, she marched over to the front door and pulled it opened, repeating her terse instruction. "Please go. Now."

Instead of leaving, Adam jerked the door out of her hand and slammed it shut. "I'm not going anywhere until you tell me what the hell you're talking about." He chose his words deliberately. "If I'm being executed, I wanted to know what you think it is I've done."

Incensed, Eve glared at him. How could he pretend to be puzzled? Had everything with him been an act? The lovemaking, the endearing words, *everything,* just an act? *This is what he does for a living. He* fools *people. And you're the biggest fool of all.*

"You don't know?" The question dripped with a sarcasm she didn't know she was capable of.

He made it a point not to lose his temper because that caused him to lose his focus, but it was a definite struggle to hold on to right now.

"No," he said evenly, "I don't know. If I knew, I wouldn't be asking you what the hell you're talking about, I'd be explaining to you just why you're wrong," he told her, praying that this was just some kind of mix-up.

"The only wrong thing I did was to fall in love with you."

He stared at her, stunned. "Wait, hold it. You're in love with me?"

She hadn't meant for that to come out. Not like this, not now. "Don't let it go to your head." She waved an impatient hand at the statement. "It doesn't change anything. I can't trust you—"

"Yes, you can," he told her with feeling. She could trust him to love her, to protect her, to be there for her forever.

But she shook her head. Because she couldn't trust him, his words to the contrary were meaningless to her. "And you don't trust me."

He was still shadowboxing in the dark. She could be referring to so many issues, things he wasn't at liberty to talk to her about yet. But soon. Until then, she was going to have to stay in limbo—about everything. "It's not a matter of trust, Eve." She had to understand that, even if he couldn't allow her into his world completely.

"Then what is it a matter of?" she demanded. "If you trusted me, you would have been straight with me from the very beginning," she insisted.

He had to know that she wouldn't have told anyone. That she would have taken his secret to the grave because she knew it could mean his life. Instead, he chose to keep her in the dark, to make her think the worst of him. He'd robbed her of the joy of sharing the stages of pregnancy with him, of life, of their combined love, growing within her.

"Do you have any idea how hard it is to know that?" she cried. "That I don't mean enough to you for you to be straight with me? To have you let me into your life and let me know what's really going on?"

He still didn't know if she thought he'd gone back to drug dealing or if this was about something else. Had Sederholm somehow gotten to her? Told her something? No, that wouldn't have been his way. The scum would have taken her hostage, not talked with her.

He didn't want her thinking of him as a pusher, but what choice did he have? This was almost over and once it was, he was free to really plead his case. If she'd listen to him.

"I told you, it's not a matter of trust. There're other things at stake. Other people at stake." Oh, the hell with it. He couldn't bear the torment in her eyes. He took hold of her shoulders and cried, "I'm not a drug dealer, Eve."

She pulled free and her anger was as fierce as ever. "I know that."

He stared at her, completely stunned. "You know that?"

"Yes," she fairly shouted. "And not because you told me, although I really, really found it hard to believe that you'd turned over a new leaf—"

He needed to have something answered. There could be really bad repercussions to this. "Then what is this about?"

"What's this about?" she echoed incredulously. He had a hell of a nerve, pretending to be in the dark. "I'll tell you what this is all about. It's about you cutting me out of your life, out of everything that's going on. It's about you not telling me that you're a government agent," she shouted at him.

He stared at her in silence for a very long moment, replaying her words in his head. "You know?"

"Yes, I know," she spat back.

"How did you find out?"

Eve lifted her chin stubbornly. So now he had questions and she had the answers. She was tempted to taunt him and ask how it felt. But she wasn't certain if Josiah would have wanted his part in this revealed, and right now, she was feeling a great deal more loyal to the older man than she was to Adam.

"It doesn't matter how I found out. The important thing is that I did—and you weren't the one to tell me."

If she knew that he wasn't a drug dealer, why was she still shouting at him? It didn't make sense. "You're angry because I'm a government agent?"

Eve was stunned by his question. Did this man have cotton for brains? "I'm angry because you didn't *tell* me you were a government agent. You let me think you werc a drug dealer."

"I couldn't compromise the operation."

She was far from placated by his answer. "But you could compromise me, what I thought of you? Do you know how many nights I spent agonizing over this? Over the fact that the father of my baby was a drug dealer? Doesn't it bother you that you could have righted everything by telling me what you were?"

Yes, it bothered him. But his hands were tied. If she knew and one of the people he was dealing with found out, a lot of lives could be lost. He couldn't take that chance.

"It wasn't my call."

He made it sound like some kind of a sporting event, not her life he was playing with. "Sorry, I didn't know the game plan ahead of time."

This wasn't getting them anywhere. He pushed past the blame portion and worked with what was. "Okay, so you know. Why are you so angry at me? I'm one of the good guys."

He might be that to others, but not to her. Not after what he'd done—or hadn't done. "No," she said very deliberately, "you are a liar. Can't you see, it doesn't matter if you're a good guy or a reformed bad guy, a lie is a lie. That's an absolute," she insisted. "And you told not one lie but two, maybe three. For all I know there are even more."

"I didn't—" Adam started to protest, but she held her hand up to stop the flow of words.

"How do I know that?" she demanded. "How do I *know* that you're not some triple agent? A bad guy pretending to be a good guy pretending to be a bad guy?"

She'd lost him for a moment. He tried to work his way backward. "Hold it—"

"No," she declared, "I won't hold it and I won't hold you. Now please, just leave," she implored, not knowing how much longer she could hold it together.

He wanted to give her some space, but he had a feeling if he walked out that door, it would be all over between them. "No, I won't leave until you tell me that we can work this out."

She shook her head, her hair bobbing about her face. "If I said that, then I would be lying just like you and I don't lie. Maybe that's stupid of me," she sniffled, "but I don't. Because I knew that a lie, *any* lie, compromises a relationship and casts doubts on it. You lied to me and now I don't know when to believe you or *if* to believe you. Fool me once, shame on you. Fool me twice, shame on me," she said, reiterating the familiar old adage. "I'm taking that to heart."

It couldn't end this way, not when he'd finally opened up his heart to someone. "Eve, please—"

But she wasn't about to be talked out of it. "I need time to think, to sort things through. I can't do it with you around."

He pressed his lips together. "Would it help if I told you I loved you?"

She didn't believe him. She wanted to, but she couldn't. "It would—if I felt I could believe you. But you could just be saying that because it's expedient right now."

He opened his mouth to argue with her, to profess his feelings more strongly, but just then, his cell phone rang. One glance at the illuminated screen told him he was getting a text message from Sederholm.

Adam bit off a curse when he saw that the deal was going down now.

She could see the struggle that was going on within him in his eyes. She made it easy for him—and for herself.

"You'd better take that," she told Adam. "It's obviously going to be more important than me."

He wanted to shout at her that nothing was more important to him than her, but he knew that the effort would be useless. He couldn't get through to her, not tonight, not given the way she felt. He'd already seen that the more he pushed, the more she resisted. As much as he didn't want to, he knew his only recourse was to pull back and let her calm down.

And then maybe, once this major drug drop came to

pass, he could devote all his attention to sorting things out *for* her.

"I'm going," he agreed. "But I'll be back." And that was a promise she could take to the bank, whether she believed him or not.

"Only if I want you to be," she informed him just before she slammed the door, cutting him off from her.

She leaned her head against the door, feeling drained. Feeling awful. God, what an idiot she'd been. Adam had to have thought of her as the most gullible person who had ever walked the earth.

Her heart ached even as she cursed him for complicating her life like this. She remained like that for a long moment, too numb to move, too unhappy to try.

Finally forcing herself to move, Eve looked at her watch. It was still early. Early enough to go pick up Brooklyn and bring her home. The thought bolstered her somewhat. She needed something to divert her, to keep her from dwelling on this overwhelming, terrible pain she felt.

Dialing Josiah's number on her cell phone, she grabbed her car keys and her purse.

He answered on the second ring. "Turner here."

"Hi, Josiah. It's Eve," she told him, heading for the front door. "There's been a change in plans. I'm coming over to pick up Brooklyn."

"Is something wrong, Eve?"

She might have known that Josiah would pick up on that. Before she could answer, the doorbell rang.

Damn it, why couldn't Adam just go away and leave her be? She didn't want to see him again, not tonight. Not for a long time.

"No, nothing's wrong," she bit off a little waspishly as she yanked open the door. Her attention switched to Adam. "Look, I said I just— Oh!"

"Eve, are you all right?" Josiah demanded. But there was no answer.

The phone had gone dead.

This didn't feel right.

The text message he'd received from Sederholm had summoned him to this location. The buy was supposed to go down within this warehouse he was standing in front of and there were no lights, no signs of life anywhere.

And, more telling, no sign of Sederholm's flashy silver Lexus convertible, the $68,000 gift, Sederholm had haughtily informed him, from the student's clueless parents for his twenty-first birthday last year.

It was a setup. It had to be.

But even as he drew out his weapon, slowly circling the perimeter of the abandoned warehouse that had once ironically housed a toy empire before it had gone bankrupt, Adam could see that something was off.

Gaining access through a side entrance that, by the looks of it, hadn't been used for some time, he moved about the darkened area slowly and cautiously. Every one of his senses was focused on the shadows as adrenaline went into high gear through his veins.

But there was no sound of breathing, no sound of movement anywhere within the warehouse. Not so much as a mouse or a rat.

Adam carefully made his way over every inch of the warehouse, moving from one wall to the other. Finding a light switch on the far wall, he held his breath and then threw it on. It wasn't powerful enough to illuminate the entire warehouse, but did highlight that he was alone.

Why would that cretin send him out on a wild goose chase?

And then it hit him. The scum had orchestrated exactly what he'd been afraid of. Sederholm had lured him away to get to Eve.

What other explanation was there?

He pulled out his cell phone to call her. But before he could, it rang in his hand. Fearing the worst, hoping for the best, he flipped it open and put it to his ear, still holding his weapon ready in his other hand.

"Hello?"

"Get back to her house!"

The voice barking the order had a slight accent. He'd only been in the man's company twice, but he recognized the voice immediately.

"Turner, what do you know?" Adam demanded.

But he found himself talking to no one. The line had gone dead. Adam didn't bother swallowing the curse that rose to his lips.

Shoving the cell phone back into his pocket, Adam quickly ran back to the rusted door that had been his point of entry into the warehouse.

Even as he flew to his vehicle, he couldn't contain the icy chill that zigzagged down his spine. He hadn't had a chance to ask Turner what this was all about, but even so, he knew.

Something was happening to Eve. And it was all his fault.

* * *

"Who the hell are you and what do you want?" Eve demanded with all the anger she could summon. The look in the young man's flat eyes made her blood run cold.

Sederholm shoved her back with the flat of his hand, while aiming his gun at her with his other. "I'm your boyfriend's playmate and I want to make sure that he doesn't think he can cut me out of the payoff that's coming." He looked around quickly to assure himself that it was just the two of them. "You think I don't know about him going behind my back, trying to make nice to my connection? *My* connection," he shouted, hitting his chest twice for emphasis. "And you're going to be my insurance policy."

She stalled for time. She'd been on the phone with Josiah. He must have heard her open the door to this stranger. If nothing else, he would be sending his driver out to check on her to see if everything was all right, the way he had when there'd been that minor earthquake in the spring.

All she needed was a split second to throw off this cocky-looking peacock. He was hardly more than a kid and she was certain he was a pushover. If he wasn't wielding a gun, she could have easily taken him, she thought, even if he had the advantage of height going for him. But her father had been thorough when she was about to go off to college and had insisted that she take lessons in self-defense. She just needed to separate this character from his weapon.

"Insurance policy against what?" she asked him, doing her best to sound interested as her mind raced around for a solution.

"I've been watching him. That bookstore owner seems to care a lot about you, sneaking off to see you when he should be working." He laid the cold steel gun barrel against her cheek, stroking it. "I'm going to make sure he thinks I'm going to hurt every pretty little hair on your head if he decides to get ahead of himself. Only room for one second-in-command and that's me."

The sound of a window opening in the rear of the house had Sederholm jerking her closer to him and wrapping an arm around her throat.

Chapter 15

The crazed intruder dragged her to the side, so that there was a wall at his back. His arm pressed down so hard against her clavicle, Eve thought she would choke to death. She could only think of Brooklyn.

Who was going to raise her daughter? Who was going to be there for the little girl when she was growing up? When she needed a mother?

She couldn't die. Her baby needed her.

Frantic, she thought of her dog, then remembered that the animal was sedated because she'd removed a benign tumor from her side. Why had she picked today of all days to do the procedure?

She had to *do* something! Clawing at her assailant's hand rather than his arm, Eve grabbed one of his fingers and bent it back as far as she could.

Sederholm howled in pain. "You bitch!" he screamed, then tightened his stranglehold even more.

Her head began to spin as she grew more and more light-headed. Desperate, she dug her nails into him. Cursing her, the man finally loosened his hold enough for her to gasp in air.

"Come on out, Smythe!" he called out. "I know you're here." His eyes scanned wildly about, unsure which way his target would enter. "Figured it out, did you? That I sent you on a wild goose chase so I could get to your whore. You're smarter than I thought. Too bad you're not as smart as me," he taunted. The almost maniacal smile disappeared as if it had never been there. "Get out here before I shoot her—because you know I will!"

Adam cursed silently.

He had to show himself. There was no other choice. Sederholm was insane enough to do just what he threatened: shoot Eve because he could.

Adam thought about coming out shooting, but he had no way of knowing exactly where Eve was in the room and he didn't want to risk hitting her. More than likely, the cowardly Sederholm held her in front of him like a shield.

Still armed, Adam positioned his weapon, ready to fire, as he emerged from the rear of the house. He saw Sederholm swing around, keeping Eve in front of him, the fireplace to his back.

"Let her go, Sederholm," he ordered, aiming his gun at the man's head. "She isn't part of this."

Sederholm shifted so that his head was partially blocked by Eve's. His voice dripped with cynicism and evil.

"Oh, on the contrary, Smythe. You care about her. That makes her a very big part of this—maybe the most important part of all."

Adam looked into Eve's eyes for a split second. Damn it, he should have never shown up on her doorstep. He should have ignored that e-mail that appeared on his computer and just concentrated on his job.

"I'm sorry," he told her.

It was too late for that. And she didn't blame him, anyway. But she needed assurance. "Just promise me you'll take care of Brooklyn."

"Brooklyn?" Sederholm interjected.

"My daughter," she responded when he jerked her hard, demanding an answer.

"Oh, right. The kid. How touching," he mocked. "What makes you think Adam here's going to be around to take care of anything?" He laid the muzzle of his gun against her temple and gazed at the man he believed was trying to take his place in the hierarchy. "Drop your gun, Smythe. Drop it or she's dead." He raised his eyebrows. "My finger feels a spasm coming on."

Terror filled her. Adam was her only chance of surviving this. "Don't do it, Adam," she pleaded. "He'll kill us both."

"Maybe," Sederholm commented. "Then again, maybe not. All depends on how I feel." His eyes challenged Adam. "I might let the pretty lady live. But not you, though. How's that for honesty?" he asked with a chilling grin. "Now put the damn gun down," he demanded, "or I swear she's dead."

Adam believed him. Very slowly, he bent his knees, placing his gun down in front of him.

"Good boy," Sederholm mocked. "Now kick it over here."

"No, don't do it, Adam," Eve cried. "Please—"

"How do you put up with this?" Sederholm asked, nodding at his hostage, his tone light as if they were two friends kicking back and shooting the breeze. Because he wanted to shut her up, Sederholm moved his arm from around her neck and quickly covered her mouth with his hand. "Now, where were we? Oh, right, I was going to shoot y—"

A shriek interrupted his sentence. Eve had bitten down on the fleshy part of his hand. Sederholm reacted automatically and pushed her from him. "You bitch!" he screamed, aiming at her.

The second Eve distracted Sederholm, Adam dived for his weapon. On the ground, his gun in his hand, Adam swiveled around, about to fire up at the drug dealer when a shot rang out through the living-room window.

Sederholm, his eyes opened wide in shock, sank down to his knees. Blood oozed from the hole between his eyes as he fell facedown on the floor.

Scrambling to his feet, adrenaline pumping, Adam whirled around toward the shattered window, ready to fire. He hadn't had time to call for any backup. This had to be Montoya, or one of the drug lord's underlings, cleaning up what had obviously become a liability for the cartel.

Out of the frying pan, into the fire. Adam backed up, using his body to shield Eve.

"You all right?" Adam tossed the question at her over his shoulder.

She struggled to keep from shaking. "Yes. But who just—?"

There was some kind of movement just beyond the window. "I think we're about to find out. Stay behind me," Adam ordered.

"Hey, don't shoot," someone called through the broken glass. "I'm not as fast as I used to be."

Eve's mouth dropped open. She recognized the voice even before the man came in. "Lucas?"

The rest of the glass from the shattered window rained into the room as it was summarily swept away. One hand raised in token surrender, Lucas came in through the window. He held a high-powered rifle in his other hand.

"That would be me," he said amiably. "Sorry about your window." He nodded toward the shattered glass on the floor. "But I didn't have time to pick my shot. I had to take what I could get."

Eve stared at the rifle. Josiah's driver seemed so comfortable with it. And there was no arguing that he was a dead shot. Wasn't anyone what they seemed?

She looked at Adam. "Is he with you?"

Adam slowly shook his head. "Not that I know of," he qualified. And then he grinned with relief. "But he can join my team anytime he wants."

Lucas laughed. "Thanks for the compliment, but I'm retired." As he spoke, he began disassembling his rifle.

This wasn't real, Eve couldn't help thinking as she watched Lucas reduce his weapon to a sum of its parts, placing each down on her coffee table. "You're not just a chauffeur, are you?"

Lucas raised his eyes to her face. "No, ma'am," he

said mildly, his fingers never missing a beat. "I'm also a cook, a social secretary whenever Mr. Turner needs one, and—"

"A sniper," Adam concluded, no question in his voice.

"No," Lucas replied easily, placing the last piece of his weaponry on the table. "I'm not a sniper. I *was* a sniper once upon a time," he admitted.

It was getting increasingly difficult to regulate her breathing. Any second now, she would need a paper bag to keep from hyperventilating.

"Does Josiah know?" Eve asked the tall, athletic man. But even as she asked, she had a feeling that she knew the answer.

Lucas's smile transformed his tanned, serious face into one belonging to a young man who enjoyed his life. "He knows."

"He sent you, didn't he?" Adam asked. It was time to get a hold of his handler. The situation could still be salvaged if they were fast enough. Digging into his pocket, he took out his phone and flipped it open.

Lucas nodded. "Mr. Turner would have come himself," he told Eve, "but his vision isn't what it used to be—and someone had to stay with the baby. I'll be right back," he promised.

Opening the front door, he stepped out for a moment. The next moment, Lucas was back, carrying what appeared to be a leather case. Laying it on the coffee table next to the rifle parts, he quickly packed the separate pieces of his weapon into it.

"If you won't be needing anything else," Lucas said, addressing his words to both of them, "I'll be getting back to the house. Mr. Turner will be anxious to debrief me."

"No, we're fine," Adam assured the older man with feeling. "Thanks to you."

Lucas smiled his thanks for the compliment and silently left.

Shaken, Eve sank down on the closest available flat surface, in this case, the coffee table. Rather than complete his call, Adam looked at her with concern. He put his hand on her shoulder. "Are you sure you're all right?"

"Peachy," she replied mechanically, staring at the inert form on her floor. "I've got a dead man in my living room, my oldest client has a driver who carries around a rifle that breaks up into tiny pieces, and my baby's father shoots people for a living." She took a deep breath and then let it out again. Nothing got better. "I've fallen down the rabbit hole and I can't get out."

Hugh could wait a few minutes. Adam closed his phone and shoved it back into his pocket. Sitting down beside Eve, he put his arm around her shoulders. She'd been through a lot tonight and he had no idea how to make it up to her.

"I'm sorry you got tangled up in this. I never wanted to get to this point, never wanted to get involved with you," he told her honestly, "because I was afraid this could happen."

She glanced up sharply, her mind still swimming. "You *knew* Lucas was going to shoot that awful man through my window?"

"No, but I was afraid that Sederholm might think of me as a threat instead of a connection to more markets and want to find some kind of leverage to use against me." He was sorrier than he could ever express. "And you were that leverage."

"Just shows-to-go-ya," she quipped, "that you can't map out everything." Eve paused a second. "Now what?"

That part was rather clear to him. "Now I call my handler and tell him what went down and then we see what we can do to salvage the sting."

Sederholm had dropped the head man's name without realizing it. It wouldn't take much for their reformed computer hacker to find where the man was staying. Once they had that information, he'd go to Montoya and make a pitch, saying he had eliminated the middle man, in this case Sederholm, and wanted to do business with the head of the cartel directly. If Montoya bought the story, the end result could still be the same.

Eve listened quietly to Adam's answer. She hadn't been talking about the operation when she'd asked. "Now what?" referred to the future of their relationship. But obviously, she and Brooklyn were far down on his list of priorities.

Eve couldn't help wondering if she'd been part of his cover. Pride kept her from asking.

"Well, good luck with that," she said as brightly as she could, standing up on very shaky legs. Her eyes were drawn to the body of the man who had come close to ter-minating her life. "Do you do clean up?" she asked Adam.

Adam took his cell phone out again. "Just getting to that."

She nodded. "Good."

Placing the call, Adam didn't notice that she clenched her fists to her sides. Eve did her best not to unleash any of the emotions running rampant through her. Because if they came out, she had no idea if she could ever bank them down again.

Because she didn't want to return to an empty house with the baby in the middle of the night, Eve waited until morning before she drove to Josiah's house to pick up her daughter. Once her arms were safely around the baby, she couldn't keep the question back any longer.

"Who are you, Josiah?"

The older man regarded her with as much of a smile as she had ever seen on his lips. "I'm your friend, Eve."

She wasn't about to engage in some sort of verbal dance, she was still much too drained from last night. "Besides that."

He considered a moment before replying, "A retired gentleman."

Not good enough. "Who was once a navy SEAL?" she demanded. "A commando?" she supplied when he made no answer. "What?"

Josiah was silent, as if debating what, if anything, to say and if so, how much. Finally, he said, "I spent time in Special Ops and then came to work for the Bureau in a rather, shall we say, unique capacity."

It had the ring of truth about it, even if a little bizarre. "Did Lucas work in the same 'unique' capacity?"

By the oddly amused expression on Josiah's face, she knew she was asking too many questions. But she needed to know. "If you're asking if that's where I met him, the answer's yes."

"Are you still part of that... 'unique' capacity?" she asked.

Josiah began to laugh. "Oh, my, no. But I do believe

that one's skills should be exercised every so often, just to keep them primed, you know." Rising, he touched her elbow, urging her to the guest bedroom where Brooklyn was sleeping. "Now take your lovely daughter and go home, Eve," he coaxed. "Lucas will follow you to make sure you get there."

"Lucas doesn't have to follow me, Josiah. I can get there on my own," she assured him. And then she paused. "Thank you for sending Lucas to my rescue."

The small shoulders lifted in a careless shrug as he walked her to the front door. "I thought your young man might need help."

So that's how Adam had managed to appear just then. Josiah had sent him, as well. "You called Adam to tell him what was going on?"

He looked at her as if to ask why she would even question such a thing. "It was only right."

Incredible. She tilted her head and kissed the older man's cheek. "Thank you."

Josiah lightly brushed the tips of his fingers along the area where she had kissed him. "My pleasure entirely, my dear," he told her with as much feeling as she'd ever heard him display.

It was over.

After months of waiting, months of preparing, months of constantly looking over his shoulder and, near the end, almost losing Eve, it was finally over.

And this time, at least, Adam thought, the good guys won.

Even so, it felt almost anticlimactic.

He supposed that was because for him, it had all

come to a head the other night, when that worthless waste of human skin had almost killed Eve. Just remembering made his stomach feel as if it was in the middle of a deadly typhoon.

Damn, but he'd earned his paycheck tonight, delivering the head man, not to mention a hell of a lot of kilos of heroin, to his boss. A lot of spoiled rich kids would have to rough it for a while, doing without their customary high.

Ordinarily, that would make *him* feel high. But he'd moved beyond that, beyond the rush a good bust brought with it. Now, in order to get that effect, he needed to have Eve beside him. Eve, making love with him. Eve, just being.

He needed to make that happen. He'd left the meeting early, letting the others celebrate. He had somewhere else to be.

As he took a sharp right, he automatically swung his hand out to keep the pizza box on the passenger seat from tumbling upside down onto the floor of the car. He didn't even remember most of the trip. He was fixated on the end goal. He hadn't spoken to her since he'd helped one of the lab boys clear out Sederholm's body. That was two days ago.

Two days felt like an eternity.

By the time he arrived at Eve's house, his heart was pounding a hell of a lot harder than it had when the final bust went down this afternoon.

Because this meant more to him.

"Here goes nothing," he murmured under his breath as he pulled up to her driveway and got out. Or rather, *everything,* he amended.

Taking the pizza box out of the car, he carried it to the front door. When he rang the doorbell, he called out, "Pizza delivery."

He was about to ring it again when the door opened.

Eve, barefoot and wearing jeans and a T-shirt, stood in the doorway, the door slightly ajar. "I didn't order any—" When she saw who it was, her mouth dropped opened. "Oh."

"No, you didn't order any," he agreed, striving to get back some of the initial charm he was supposed to have had. "But I thought you might want to celebrate."

She slanted a look at him. "Just what is it that I'm celebrating?"

"Well, the almost perfect drug bust for one," he told her. He knew it sounded like a boast, but he deserved to give himself a little praise. "As of this afternoon, there's going to be a lot less heroin on the street, at least for the time being."

"You said 'for one,'" she reminded him. "What's 'for two?'"

He studied her for a long moment. For two cents, he'd sweep her into his arms and just head for the hills. But he knew she'd never be happy with that. She thrived in crowds, around people. And he loved anything that made Eve Eve.

"Two is a little trickier," he admitted.

Now he had her curious. "What is it?" she wanted to know.

He put his hand up, as if to say all in good time. "Before I answer that, I need to spread these out."

Eve watched as he laid out what looked like old report cards on the kitchen table. Her eyes narrowed as she looked at the one closest to her. "Are those report cards?"

"Yes. Mine," he added before she could ask.

Just to verify the unusual claim, Eve picked one up and glanced over it. It was his all right. And he was a fairly decent student, she noted. She put the card back on the counter. "Why are you showing me your old report cards?"

"So you can see that I mean it when I tell you that for you, I intend my life to be an open book. I'll show you anything you want to look at," he promised. "No more secrets, Eve. Not from you. I want you to know everything there is to know about me."

This all sounded well and good, but she wasn't going to allow herself to get carried away or let her imagination run wild. She wanted everything spelled out.

"Because?" she prodded.

"Because," he began evenly, "then you can't use the excuse that I'm keeping things from you."

He certainly didn't believe in shooting straight from the shoulder. "And why would I want an excuse?"

"To use in case you want to turn me down," he told her, hating the very thought.

She almost felt like throwing up her hands. Almost. "You know, maybe it's your secret agent mentality that makes you think this convoluted way, but I've always found that the simplest path between two points is a straight line. Draw me a straight line, Adam," she implored. "What are you trying to say?"

"Actually," he corrected, "I'm trying to *ask* something."

She dug deep for patience. "Okay, what are you trying to ask? Spit it out, Adam," she ordered briskly.

So he did. "Will you marry me?"

It took her a second to come to. A second more to breathe evenly. "That depends."

He didn't understand. "On what?"

"On who's asking me," she told him, then specified her problem. "Is it Adam Smythe or Adam Serrano who wants to marry me?"

"It's just me," he told her softly, taking her hand and placing it against his heart. "Adam. Just Adam. And just so you know," he interjected before she could answer, "no matter what your answer is, I plan to love you for the rest of my life."

She could feel her heart melting in her chest.

"Well, Just Adam," she began, smiling at him, "I can't see how I can resist a proposal like that."

He laughed and hugged her close. "I was hoping you'd see it that way. Any chance that I could have a do-over on that romantic evening you were planning for us the other night?"

"You mean the night your little playdate pal tried to kill me?"

He had the good grace to wince. "That's the one."

Eve wrapped her arms around his neck and raised her face up to his. Her eyes were smiling. "Every chance in the world."

"That's what I wanted to hear," Adam murmured just before he sealed the deal with a long, soulful kiss that promised to go on forever.

And nearly did.

Epilogue

Laura Delaney pushed herself away from her computer for a moment. Not to get up, just to reflect.

A very self-satisfied smile curved her lips as she closed her eyes and savored the message she'd just read in her private e-mail account. The one that she still maintained for communications that involved the life she had once led, not her life now. Her contact at the CIA had just informed her that not only had Adam Serrrano shown up on Eve's doorstep to take responsibility for the child she was carrying, he'd actually helped deliver said child and then stuck around to marry Eve. The two now appeared to be the very definition of happiness.

Mission accomplished.

She'd never thought the old, familiar term would

feel so good to her. Sound so good to her. Heaven knew that she didn't regret leaving the Company. But she did miss that sense that all was right with the world that came over her when a mission resolved itself well. That feeling was there now, in spades. She'd set out to reunite Eve with her lover and she had. Moreover, it had turned out even better than she'd hoped. The magic that had brought them together in the first place hadn't faded. It had only grown stronger, despite the obstacles.

Would that ever happen to her? She'd like to think so, but she was realistic enough to know that most likely, she would never get the chance to find out. Finding the location of the father of her son had proven to be impossible up until now. There was no reason to believe that would change despite her efforts and the combined efforts of her old friends at the Company. God knew she'd tried.

Don't spoil your mood. You did good. Maybe, just maybe, if you put your mind to it, you can do good again. You seem to have a lot better luck locating unsuspecting fathers when they don't directly involve you.

Laura smiled again and opened her eyes. It was late, but she wasn't sleepy. Jeremy was tucked away in bed, sleeping like a little rock and she didn't much feel like watching TV tonight. The holiday season presented nothing but reruns on its schedule tonight.

Time to see if she could get lightning to strike twice.

Pulling up close to the computer again, she went back to the Web site she'd originally set up to network with other single mothers. She was curious to see if there was anything in her in-box.

A few strokes brought her to the right location. She

moved her cursor over the e-mail button and clicked it.
The screen filled up with unread mail.

Settling in, Laura smiled to herself. Time to get busy.
MysteryMom had work to do.

* * * * *

Don't miss the next romance in this series,
THE COWBOY'S SECRET TWINS,
by Carla Cassidy, available November 2009 from
Silhouette Romantic Suspense.

The helicopter swung abruptly sideways in a dizzying arch, setting Jack McCall's fever-ravaged brain spinning.

His friend's voice sounded tinny, coming through the earphones. "You belong in a hospital," he said. "Not some backwater bed-and-breakfast."

All Jack really knew about the virus raging through his system was that it wasn't contagious, and there was no known treatment for it besides a lot of rest and quiet. "I don't like hospitals," he responded, hoping he sounded like his normal self. "They're full of sick people."

Vince Griffin chuckled but it was a dry sound, rough at the edges. "What's in Stone Creek, Arizona?" he asked. "Besides a whole lot of nothin'?"

Ashley O'Ballivan was in Stone Creek, and she was a whole lot of somethin', but Jack had neither the strength nor the inclination to explain. After the way he'd ducked out six months before, he didn't expect a welcome, knew he didn't deserve one. But Ashley, being Ashley, would take him in whatever her misgivings.

He had to get to Ashley; he'd be all right.

He closed his eyes, letting the fever swallow him.

There was no telling how much time had passed when he became aware of the chopper blades slowing overhead. Dimly, he saw the private ambulance waiting on the airfield outside of Stone Creek; it seemed that twilight had descended.

Jack sighed with relief. His clothes felt clammy against his flesh. His teeth began to chatter as two figures unloaded a gurney from the back of the ambulance and waited for the blades to stop.

"Great," Vince remarked, unsnapping his seat belt. "Those two look like volunteers, not real EMTs."

The chopper bounced sickeningly on its runners, and Vince, with a shake of his head, pushed open his door and jumped to the ground, head down.

Jack waited, wondering if he'd be able to stand on his own. After fumbling unsuccessfully with the buckle on his seat belt, he decided not.

When it was safe the EMTs approached, following Vince, who opened Jack's door.

His old friend Tanner Quinn stepped around Vince, his grin not quite reaching his eyes.

"You look like hell warmed over," he told Jack cheerfully.

"Since when are you an EMT?" Jack retorted.

Tanner reached in, wedged a shoulder under Jack's

right arm and hauled him out of the chopper. His knees immediately buckled, and Vince stepped up, supporting him on the other side.

"In a place like Stone Creek," Tanner replied, "everybody helps out."

They reached the wheeled gurney, and Jack found himself on his back.

Tanner and the second man strapped him down, a process that brought back a few bad memories.

"Is there even a hospital in this place?" Vince asked irritably from somewhere in the night.

"There's a pretty good clinic over in Indian Rock," Tanner answered easily, "and it isn't far to Flagstaff." He paused to help his buddy hoist Jack and the gurney into the back of the ambulance. "You're in good hands, Jack. My wife is the best veterinarian in the state."

Jack laughed raggedly at that.

Vince muttered a curse.

Tanner climbed into the back beside him, perched on some kind of fold-down seat. The other man shut the doors.

"You in any pain?" Tanner said as his partner climbed into the driver's seat and started the engine.

"No." Jack looked up at his oldest and closest friend and wished he'd listened to Vince. Ever since he'd come down with the virus—a week after snatching a five-year-old girl back from her non-custodial parent, a small-time Colombian drug dealer—he hadn't been able to think about anyone or anything but Ashley. When he *could* think, anyway.

Now, in one of the first clearheaded moments he'd experienced since checking himself out of Bethesda the day before, he realized he might be making a major mistake. Not by facing Ashley—he owed her that much and a lot more. No, he could be putting her in danger, putting Tanner and his daughter and his pregnant wife in danger, too.

"I shouldn't have come here," he said, keeping his voice low.

Tanner shook his head, his jaw clamped down hard as though he was irritated by Jack's statement.

"This is where you belong," Tanner insisted. "If you'd had sense enough to know that six months ago, old buddy, when you bailed on Ashley without so much as a fare-thee-well, you wouldn't be in this mess."

Ashley. The name had run through his mind a million times in those six months, but hearing somebody say it out loud was like having a fist close around his insides and squeeze hard.

Jack couldn't speak.

Tanner didn't press for further conversation.

The ambulance bumped over country roads, finally hitting smooth blacktop.

"Here we are," Tanner said. "Ashley's place."

* * * * *

Will Jack be able to patch things up with Ashley,
or will his past put the woman he loves
in harm's way?
Find out in
AT HOME IN STONE CREEK
by Linda Lael Miller
Available November 2009 from
Silhouette Special Edition®

**This November,
Silhouette Special Edition®
brings you**

NEW YORK TIMES
BESTSELLING AUTHOR

LINDA LAEL
MILLER

At Home in
Stone Creek

*Available in November
wherever books are sold.*

NEW YORK TIMES BESTSELLING AUTHOR

SHARON SALA

THE DAUGHTER OF A FORBIDDEN LOVE COMES HOME....

As a legacy of hatred erupts in a shattering moment of violence, a dying mother entrusts her newborn daughter to a caring stranger. Now, twenty-five years later, Katherine Fane has come home to Camarune, Kentucky, to bury the woman who'd raised her, bringing a blood feud to its searing conclusion.

At the cabin in the woods where she was born, Katherine is drawn to the ravaged town and its violent past. But her arrival has not gone unnoticed. A stranger is watching from the woods, a shattered old man is witnessing the impossible, and Sheriff Luke DePriest's only thoughts are to keep Katherine safe from the sleeping past she has unwittingly awoken....

THE RETURN

Available September 29, 2009, wherever books are sold!

nocturne™

TIME RAIDERS
THE PROTECTOR

by *USA TODAY* bestselling author
MERLINE LOVELACE

Former USAF officer Cassandra Jones's unique psychic
skills come in handy, as she has been selected to join the
elite Time Raiders squad. Her first mission is to travel
back to seventh-century China to locate the final piece
of a missing bronze medallion. Major Max Brody is
assigned to accompany her, and soon Cassandra and
Max have to fight their growing attraction to each
other while the mission suddenly turns deadly....

*Available November
wherever books are sold.*

SN61822

REQUEST YOUR FREE BOOKS!

2 FREE NOVELS PLUS 2 FREE GIFTS!

Silhouette® Romantic

SUSPENSE

Sparked by Danger, Fueled by Passion!

YES! Please send me 2 FREE Silhouette® Romantic Suspense novels and my 2 FREE gifts (gifts are worth about $10). After receiving them, if I don't wish to receive any more books, I can return the shipping statement marked "cancel." If I don't cancel, I will receive 4 brand-new novels every month and be billed just $4.24 per book in the U.S. or $4.99 per book in Canada. That's a savings of at least 15% off the cover price! It's quite a bargain! Shipping and handling is just 50¢ per book*. I understand that accepting the 2 free books and gifts places me under no obligation to buy anything. I can always return a shipment and cancel at any time. Even if I never buy another book from Silhouette, the two free books and gifts are mine to keep forever.

240 SDN EYL4   340 SDN EYMG

Name _____ (PLEASE PRINT) _____

Address _____ Apt. # _____

City _____ State/Prov. _____ Zip/Postal Code _____

Signature (if under 18, a parent or guardian must sign) _____

Mail to the **Silhouette Reader Service:**
IN U.S.A.: P.O. Box 1867, Buffalo, NY 14240-1867
IN CANADA: P.O. Box 609, Fort Erie, Ontario L2A 5X3

Not valid to current subscribers of Silhouette Romantic Suspense books.

Want to try two free books from another line?
Call 1-800-873-8635 or visit www.morefreebooks.com.

* Terms and prices subject to change without notice. Prices do not include applicable taxes. Sales tax applicable in N.Y. Canadian residents will be charged applicable provincial taxes and GST. Offer not valid in Quebec. This offer is limited to one order per household. All orders subject to approval. Credit or debit balances in a customer's account(s) may be offset by any other outstanding balance owed by or to the customer. Please allow 4 to 6 weeks for delivery. Offer available while quantities last.

Your Privacy: Silhouette is committed to protecting your privacy. Our Privacy Policy is available online at www.eHarlequin.com or upon request from the Reader Service. From time to time we make our lists of customers available to reputable third parties who may have a product or service of interest to you. If you would prefer we not share your name and address, please check here. ☐

SRS09R

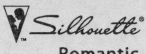

Silhouette®

Romantic
SUSPENSE

**Sparked by Danger,
Fueled by Passion.**

*Blackout
At Christmas*

Beth Cornelison,
Sharron McClellan,
Jennifer Morey

What happens when a major blackout shuts
down the entire Western seaboard on Christmas
Eve? Follow stories of danger, intrigue and
romance as three women learn to trust their
instincts to survive and open their hearts to the
love that unexpectedly comes their way.

**Available November
wherever books are sold.**

Silhouette® Romantic

SUSPENSE

COMING NEXT MONTH

Available October 27, 2009

#1583 BLACKOUT AT CHRISTMAS
"Stranded with the Bridesmaid" by Beth Cornelison
"Santa Under Cover" by Sharron McClellan
"Kiss Me on Christmas" by Jennifer Morey
In these short stories, three couples find themselves stranded in a city-wide blackout during a Christmas Eve blizzard.

#1584 THE COWBODY'S SECRET TWINS—Carla Cassidy
Top Secret Deliveries
All Henry Randolf wants for Christmas is to be left alone. But Melissa Morgan shows up at his Texas ranch with adorable twin boys—quite clearly *his* twin boys—and he knows his life will never be the same. When a crazed killer puts the new family in his sights, Henry and Melissa must learn to work together—for their love and for the safety of their boys.

#1585 HIS WANTED WOMAN—Linda Turner
The O'Reilly Brothers
As a special agent, Patrick O'Reilly always has to put duty before desire. But his current suspect, Mackenzie Sloan, is tempting him beyond belief. Her eyes assert her innocence, though the evidence is against her. Will Patrick decide to trust his head...or his heart?

#1586 IMMINENT AFFAIR—Sheri WhiteFeather
Warrior Society
The first time warrior Daniel Deer Runner met Allie Whirlwind, he was injured saving her life. Now there are gaps in Daniel's memory—a memory that includes falling in love with Allie. But when Allie's in danger again, he's hell-bent on protecting her. Will their old feelings resurface before time runs out?